THE BOY IN THE HOODIE
I0827354

The Boy in the Hoodie

Published by Rhiza Press
PO BOX 1519
Capalaba QLD 4157
Australia

Cover Design by Carmen Dougherty

National Library of Australia Cataloguing-in-Publication entry:

Creator: Mckeown, Catriona, author.
Title: The boy in the hoodie / Catriona Mckeown.
ISBN: 9781925563207 (paperback)
Subjects: Friendship--Fiction.

Catriona McKeown

For Larry

Chapter 1

Before I met him, there wasn't much I knew about the boy in the hoodie. He seemed to live above the rules, allowed to get away with the most astonishing things in class. He'd never do any work; he'd just draw these dark charcoal sketches all the time. Looking back, I know drawing was a way to help him deal with stuff. Just like how, in writing, I'm learning to deal with my own stuff, my own way. My psychologist said writing the story will help me heal. My left shoulder is still stiff; I can't turn it in a full circle without pain shooting out through my muscles, down my arm and into my back. But I know that's not the healing she means. She means the healing I need so I don't keep waking up during the night in a sweat, my heart racing and tears gushing down my face, but with no memory of why. Or how, instead of my face in the mirror, I see dark eyes peering out from under a grey hoodie.

I'm just hoping that, maybe, getting the story out of my head and onto my laptop might mean I stop thinking about what happened to us. Because I do, all the time.

It was just over five months ago when I first remember taking notice of the new boy at school—the one who constantly wore a hoodie pulled up over his head. It was the same day my best friend, Megan, finished up at Central High to go to a new private school in The Bay. It had been one of the worst days of my life. I'd been dreading it ever since Megan announced she'd applied for a scholarship there. On her own. *Without me.*

And it wasn't as though I'd never smelled alcohol before. I had, plenty of times—on Grandpa's breath when we'd kiss hello, on his clothes, his hands, the glass he drank from. But that lunch break, when I sniffed the bottle that Paige passed around, I didn't pick it as alcohol. I guess not all alcohol smells the same.

Paige had us sitting around in a circle as though we were preparing to play some kids' game like pass-the-parcel. It wasn't our usual sitting place as it was no ordinary occasion. My heart thumped in my chest with such force I was sure the other girls must have been able to hear it.

'In honour of Megan's leaving us for a better place,' Paige had said, sitting up straight, a stainless-steel, hot pink drink bottle resting where her shins met, 'I've brought a little something special for us to share.'

Paige was adult-beautiful. Her blonde hair flowed across her face in waves like she'd just stepped out of a shampoo commercial. Even the pink-tipped ends somehow failed to clash with our maroon school uniform. And she had blue eyes that sparkled like glitter when she smiled—at least they did back then.

I would have given anything to have her eyes, rather than my own pale-blue-in-fact-almost-grey eyes. I ran my hand over my limp ponytail, feeling its lifelessness with every fingertip. Not quite blonde, but certainly not brown. I hated everything about my hair. I swallowed hard. Paige looked so sweet and innocent, but I didn't trust her; experience warned me Paige was setting us up for something I wasn't going to like.

'I thought we should share a special drink'—Paige held the bottle up as though it was something to worship—'as a kind of soldiery pack to send Megan on her way.'

I looked at Paige blankly.

'Do you mean solidarity pact?' Megan asked.

Paige rolled her eyes. 'Whatever.' She flicked her hair over her shoulder and flashed a flirty smile. 'As we drink from the one bottle'—she held the bottle straight out before her—'let's remember that no matter where we are, we're in this together. Teachers are the same no matter what school we go to. It's us or them. And we choose us, always.' She unscrewed the lid. Her lips barely brushed the bottle's mouthpiece as she poured the off-white, milky liquid into her mouth.

While Megan was my best friend, Paige was the leader of our little group. I won't deny that I had only stayed friends with Paige because, in being her friend, I held position in our year level: not one of the popular girls, but not a friendless plebe, either. Don't get me wrong, I liked Paige—I still do, after everything. She was messed up for sure, but sometimes she could be the most amazing and fun person to be with.

What I get now is, Paige and I were preparing to walk different life paths. I was the pastor's kid, a 'good' student that teachers pretty much left alone. My parents loved this side of me, which made my life at home okay. Paige hated it, which caused problems sometimes, but never anything to stop us being friends. I'm pretty sure it was only because we'd been friends since primary school that she allowed me to stay in the group. But I didn't mind because Paige was beautiful, and kind of a free spirit. I was just acceptable. High school can be brutal, but knowing the right people makes it bearable.

Keira smiled as she took the bottle from Paige and after giving the bottle a little shake, smelled it. 'Mmm chocolate,' she said, winking at Paige. Keira had the most amazing eyelashes. They were so long they moved in the breeze, making her brown eyes look as though they were dancing. She was Paige's best friend but she was my friend as well.

We kind of looked after Paige together, tried to stop her from doing anything too stupid, if you know what I mean. Or at least it used to be like that—once we got to middle school, Paige seemed to do whatever she wanted, regardless of what I thought.

Paige motioned for Keira to have a drink, and she took a sip like Paige had, as though they'd done this sort of thing together before. She looked a little strangely at Paige, who grinned like a lioness watching her family devour the meal she'd just caught. I swallowed hard as they began whispering behind their hands, giggling.

I could feel heat growing up my neck and spreading like a disease across my face. Why couldn't I hide my emotions like a normal teenager? I glanced up at the gum trees, and silently prayed the shadows they were casting were enough to hide my discomfort. There had to be more than just some sort of chocolate milk in the bottle.

I wiped clammy hands down my checkered school dress. 'You know, Megs, you're so lucky to be going to a new school,' I whispered, pulling my socks up higher to stop the grass irritating my legs, trying to ignore what was happening with the bottle beside me. 'You'll have the rest of Year Nine to make some awesome new friends and be all set for senior school next year.'

'Yeah, but I'm missing out on the middle school graduation dinner . That completely sucks.'

'It's just a stupid dinner.' I picked at the grass, holding back the tears threatening to spill. I was already dreading going to the dinner without Megan. Keira and Paige would hang out together all night—I'd be the third wheel. And some boy asking me to be their date to the dinner was about as likely as Cinderella and Prince Charming actually living happily ever after. 'I'm happy for you'—I attempted a smile at Megan—'but, school already sucks enough. I can't imagine how awful it's going to be without you here.'

Megan's eyes seemed to be following the bottle.

'Have you asked your parents about coming to St Andrew's next year?'

'My parents can't afford it, you know.' I hung my head low. 'Besides, I'd still have to survive the rest of the year here without you.'

'Yeah, but it would be doable, wouldn't it?'

I shrugged. What did it matter? I was never going to St Andrew's. It was public schooling the whole way for me.

'You've got to hold on to our plan, Kat.' Megan squeezed my hand. 'We'll find a way for you to go to St Andrew's, too. Don't give up hoping.' I looked back out over the school oval, a cool breeze trying its best to rustle the grass that was beginning to die—winter had brought hardly any rain. If only I could get out of this place. The grass was sure to be greener at St Andrew's—they could probably afford sprinklers, and the water rates to go with them.

'Right, girls. Your turn. Come on, Megan, have a taste.' Paige pushed the bottle into Megan's chest.

Megan screwed up her nose.

'You have to,' Paige said, pouting. 'It's my little farewell gift to you.'

Megan took the bottle and I heard her breathe in deeply. She held the bottle to her lips. Her hand wobbled and the metallic pink turned her left cheek red as she hesitate. As Megan gulped in the 'milk', I watched her eyes widen and she looked for a moment like she might spit it back out. They began watering as she placed the bottle gently on the ground. She gave Paige a strange look.

'Isn't it great?' Paige raised her eyebrows, her face alight with an elated smile.

Megan didn't say anything.

Paige picked up the bottle and thrust it into my hands. 'Your turn, Mary.'

'Mary' was the name Paige called me when she thought I was being a suck-up, not taking chances, or not joining in on some risky adventure she had concocted. 'Mary' was her way of giving me no choice but to go along on one of her reckless schemes. It was a threat—*join in, or suffer the fate.*

My stomach sat at the bottom of my throat as I took the bottle and brought it to my mouth. I couldn't smell anything but chocolate milk. For a moment, my muscles relaxed.

I slowly tipped the bottle back. My lips warmed and a deep heat flowed down the back of my throat. It was a weird feeling, a weird taste. Not disgusting, but nothing like I'd tasted before. I didn't like it. But I didn't hate it, either.

A great mass of cloud descended as the realisation of what I had just done filled my head. I had sipped from Paige's drink bottle. I had drunk…*what?*

Paige grabbed the bottle off me and swore under her breath. 'You guys are gutless. You need to take a good swig of it, like this.' She raised the bottle to her lips and took a couple of big gulps of the milky liquid.

Megan spoke the words that were moving around my head like a huge freight train: big, heavy. 'Is that, like, alcohol or something?' She coughed a little as she spoke.

Paige nodded. 'Did you actually think I'd brought a chocolate milkshake to see you off to your fancy private school?'

I put my head down. I clawed my way through the fog in my brain and remembered having thought that exact thought. Well, I may have considered it, but I don't think I ever believed it. It was a cute thought, that a chocolate milkshake could have been the delicious surprise Paige had brought for us to share.

But no, she brought us alcohol. Her mum's favourite, she'd said. Paige took another swig, then passed it around for us all to drink from again. Keira and Megan took bigger sips this time.

I waited my turn with a dry mouth. I tried to convince myself that I had a choice; I didn't have to drink it again. Surely, if I chose not to take another sip, my friends would understand. And with time, they would forgive me. Eventually, we'd move on.

But then again, would it hurt to have another sip? No one else would ever know. It could be our group's secret; a stupid story to laugh about.

There was more than one way that this scenario could play out, but which choice—*to drink or not to drink*—had the least consequences?

The bottle was pretty much empty by the time it got back to me. Only one mouthful left, at best. I toyed with the bottle for a moment, looking at it, rolling it in the palms of my hands. Three sets of eyes watched me. I could see the word forming on Paige's lips: *Mary*. Her narrowed eyes were telling me to hurry up and drink it. I stared down at the bottle. The first sip, I hadn't known what I was doing. This time, I'd be knowingly drinking alcohol at school.

And so, when Mr Wally walked around from behind the row of pine trees that lined the school boundary, I froze. It hadn't occurred to me to empty the bottle, to tip it over, even just to hide it behind my back. I had still been in the process of deciding whether I was even going to sip from it again.

I'd never been good at getting caught out. Mum reckoned she could always tell when I was guilty even before she asked the question.

Why exactly Mr Wally felt the need to inspect the bottle, I don't know. Maybe it was Paige's reputation. Maybe there was a smell in the air. Maybe it was the bewildered look on my face. But suddenly I was being marched towards the principal's office.

And Mr Wally had a bright pink drink bottle in his hand, with my fingerprints all over it.

CHAPTER 2

The four of us sat in the school corridor out the front of Principal Dean's office. We were spaced out along the wooden bench reserved only for students who had got into super bad trouble.

I desperately wiped my palms down the front of my school dress, trying to dry them, trying to remove the sweat, the smell, the droplets of the forbidden substance that may or may not have splashed onto them while I held that bottle. My veins were pulsating in my neck in a way that I hadn't experienced since the night Mum woke me up to tell me she was taking Dad to hospital because he had chest pain.

Paige, Keira and Megan were talking, whispering, while I sat in stunned silence. There were drawings pinned to the walls all the way down the corridor. They were so sweet; innocent drawings of Grade Sevens' self-portraits, with weird looking eyes and disproportionate foreheads. I longed to be back in Grade Seven. Life was so much simpler then, so much easier.

I'd never really been in trouble before. This was my first time on the principal's bench. Even though I was friends with Paige—who was arguably one of the most troubled kids in school—I'd managed to avoid getting dragged into anything that sent me to Mr Dean's office. Until today…

Paige handed the other two girls something, which they

fiddled with before putting it in their mouths. Peppermint filled the air. I waited for Paige to hand one to me, but she put the packet back in her pocket. I frowned. 'What about me?'

The three girls exchanged a look. Megan shuffled closer beside me so her thigh pressed against mine, even though there was plenty of room on the bench. She looked across at Paige and Keira, who nodded, and then looked at me.

'What?'

'Kat,' Megan's voice was so quiet I could hardly hear it. 'We've been talking.'

Keira had her head down, looking at the floor as though it was of spectacular interest. Paige looked directly at me, into my eyes. If she had a gift of communicating telepathically, she'd have accomplished it at that moment. Her eyes were screaming at me something of the utmost importance.

'We think you should take the fall for this,' Megan said. Keira chewed noisily as the white piece of gum floated around in her open mouth. Paige elbowed her and she scowled before closing her mouth.

'Wait—who, me?'

The three girls nodded.

'I'll get expelled, Kat,' Paige said. 'They won't let me back into the school after this. If they find out I brought alcohol into the school yard, and offered it to you guys, they'll throw the book at me. And who'll have me then? Where will I go if I can't go here?'

I knew better than to answer her, even though we all knew there were two other state schools in Fairview. I knew what Paige meant, though, and it was true; there'd be no probation period this time. She'd be told to pack her bag and not come back. Then it would only be me and Keira left.

Keira's auburn-dyed hair was tied back into pigtails, but the innocent look on her face didn't fool me. Had this been her idea to save Paige from getting into trouble?

'Kat, if I took the fall'—her brown eyes welled with tears—'Mum'd kill me. She's already got Harriet and Mia grounded for a month, plus Jenna's on her final probation for stealing her teacher's phone and sending rude text messages to random numbers. I'm the good one. If I go down for this, it'll send Mum to the dark side. I can't do it to her. But we can't let Paige take the fall for this, either. She was doing it for Megan—to give her a send-off to remember. We can't make her take the blame when she was doing something great for us all.' Tears spilt down Keira's cheeks. She'd had a tough couple of years, what with her dad leaving and her mum not coping real well on her own.

I nodded. 'Maybe. But we could have waited until after school.'

Paige rolled her eyes. 'Ya Mary.'

I glared back at her before turning to Megan, my *bestest friend* in the whole world. And yes, I was going to ask her the question, despite the nauseated knot that squirmed in the pit of my stomach. Surely *she* wouldn't leave me on my own in this.

'Megs? You're leaving, anyway.' But even Megan shook her head. 'Paige reckons Mr Dean would be obliged to pass the information on to my next school and they'd cancel the scholarship in a flash. I can't take the risk. I can't. I'm sorry.'

Megan placed her hand on mine as the realisation of what was being said dropped like a thick, wet woolen blanket on my shoulders. It hurt. It tasted like sour worms that made my face contort as I sucked on them.

'But what about our plan?' I was desperately holding back the lump growing in my throat. 'How can I follow you to St Andrew's if I have this on my record?'

Megan shook her head. 'I really want you to come to St

Andrew's with me, Kat, but this might mean I don't get to go there, either. What would be the point then?'

It was all down to this: me with the truth, or them...my friends.

I looked again at the three faces before me, and refused to accept the verdict. I did not want to take the fall for this. What if one day I had the chance to go to Megan's fancy private school on a scholarship for something too? Sure, I was yet to discover any hidden talents that could get me in for free—but the chances of a school like that giving a scholarship to someone with this kind of blotch on their record was next to none. This was my whole future we were playing with.

'We could take the blame together, Keira,' I said. 'My parents aren't exactly going to be dancing with joy about me drinking at school, either. And besides, you had more to drink than me. What's to say they won't be just as lenient on you as me?'

'I don't exactly have a clear record, remember.' Keira's eyes narrowed before turning back to focus on an invisible object on the floor. She swore under her breath. 'You have to take the blame, Kat. It's your fault we're here.'

'Yeah, Kat. You just sat there like an idiot.' Paige's teeth clenched together as she spoke. 'You should have dumped the contents, knocked it over or something.'

I shook my head. I'd hardly had time to do anything.

'Yeah, or you could have just finished the bottle off,' Keira said. 'While Mr Wally was saying goodbye to Megan, you just sat there, staring at him. You might as well have stood up and breathed in his face, yelling, "Hey, I'm in the middle of breaking a really big school rule".'

'It's true,' Paige said. 'You had the chance to save us from all this and you blew it. Big time.

I looked at Megan—her eyes were sad. She was looking past me, down the corridor to the large double doors. They were her doors of freedom, not mine. I would have to see this year out behind these walls. And even if I wanted to go to one of the other state schools in town, my choices were limited. I could end up being more alone than ever.

'I'm really sorry, Kat. You know I would own up to it too, if I could. But it would be easy for you to take the blame.' Megan wouldn't look at me as she spoke. 'You were the one they found holding the bottle.' She ran her fingers across her mouth as she spoke. 'It would be easy to say it was only you who'd been drinking it.'

She might as well have punched me in the stomach when she said those words. Megan knew Mr Dean and his wife went to the church where my dad was the pastor—a fact none of my other friends knew. She had to realise there was more than just school stuff at stake for me. 'No, I don't want to do this. It's not fair. And it's not even my bottle—it's Paige's.' My fingers gripped tightly to the bench seat. 'Mr Dean would never believe me. Why would I bring alcohol to school?'

'Do you think I'm stupid enough,' Paige said through a clenched jaw, 'to bring alcohol to school in a bottle with my name on it? Of course you can say it's yours. Make something up. Say you got it for your birthday or something.'

'My birthday that is next month?' As if she didn't know that. My birthday's only a few weeks after hers. 'Besides, they'll want to know why we were hiding behind the pine trees. It looks suspicious. I'm a terrible liar. We won't get away with it.'

'We will,' Paige said, 'if we all go in with the same story. We need to find a lesser crime and admit that was why we were behind the trees. Only you'll be admitting to the alcohol.'

'We could say we were planning a teacher prank on Mrs Henderson as a send-off for Megan and didn't want to be overheard?' Keira said.

'Great idea. And, Mary'—Paige's eyes narrowed—'you'll need to come up with your own story. Say something like your dad's heart is stuffed again and with Megan leaving, you're not coping. They'll feel sorry you. They'll give you a probation, probably suggest a few counselling sessions with the psych. Nothing too rash.' Paige's face softened and she looked at me sympathetically, as though the decision had already been made. 'The teachers like your type, Kat. They'll go easy on you. Make sure you shed some tears; you'll have them eating out of your hand.'

I found myself nodding, though the heaviness in my stomach was making me nauseous. I could feel the alcohol burning inside me, destroying me from the inside out.

The door to the principal's office opened. Paige tapped Keira and Megan, and I watched them swallow the gum in their mouths. My hands started shaking. Was I really agreeing to lie to Mr Dean?

A boy with a grey hoodie pulled up over his head walked out of Mr Dean's office and shut the door behind him. I sighed, relieved. But before long that door would be opening again, and this time it would be for me.

'Hey, there's that new boy. The creep,' Keira said.

'What's he doing in Mr Dean's office?' Paige asked loud enough that the boy would be able to hear. He peeked out from under the hoodie that was hiding dark eyes and looked at Paige with a snarl.

'Geez, Paige, what's he got against you?' Keira asked.

Paige shrugged. 'He's a freak. Goes on my bus sometimes, but he just sits there and stares out the window. He never speaks to anyone except the bus driver. What can I say? He makes good target practice.'

'What do you throw at him?' I asked.

Paige shrugged. 'Whatever we have on us.'

I watched him with curiosity. He walked with his shoulders bent forward, his hands plunged into the pockets of his hoodie, his Vans barely lifting from the lino. I suspected he would be reasonably tall for a Year Nine boy, if he pulled his shoulders back and stood up straight.

He was only a few metres away from us when he turned and pointed at Paige with his middle finger, before turning it up towards the ceiling. I gasped a little—he looked so natural in the way he raised his finger like that, walking along, as though it were the most ordinary thing in the world to do.

'Jerk.' Paige gave the gesture back, even though he was no longer looking at her. 'Who does he think he is?'

'I heard his mum was killed by the Mafia,' Keira said. 'And his dad is in jail on death row, so the kid had to move here to stay with some relatives.'

'We don't have death row in Australia,' Megan said.

'Well, who even cares.' Keira picked at something on her school jumper. 'Suzie in 9K says he always rocks up to form late and then sits down the back, watching everyone. Such a crank.'

'He's in our advanced math class, isn't he?' I asked Megan. 'He seemed pretty quiet to me.'

Megan shivered. 'I hope they expel him or something.' We all looked at her. 'For your sakes, I mean. You don't want someone with that kind of history in your school, do you?'

The re-opening of Principal Dean's office door brought my attention back to the present problem. He asked us all to stand up. I wondered if my knees would hold me. It was all I could do to stop them from twitching as he walked past us, his nose so close to my face I could smell the coffee on his breath. He stopped in front of me, before looking back over the other girls with a frown. A tingling chill rolled down my back. 'Kat, I will see you first, please.'

With lead feet, I walked the few metres to his office. I turned and looked at my friends who gave encouraging smiles. My friends—the three girls who were sitting back, watching me walk the plank alone. Mr Dean coughed. My heart was beating so fast I thought it might leap out of my mouth if I dared to open it.

The look on Mr Dean's face was worse than the anger I'd expected—it was disappointment. I wouldn't have to worry about making myself cry.

CHAPTER 3

Mr Dean indicated for me to take a seat in a plastic chair directly in front of his large wooden desk. I pulled my jumper sleeves down over my hands as I clasped them firmly in my lap. I dared not look up. If I looked up into Mr Dean's face, I knew I would start blubbering. I had to hold myself together.

I could hear Mr Dean sitting down in his chair, the wheels moving across the floorboards as he pulled himself closer to the desk. Writing implements rattled in a jar and there was the opening and closing of a drawer. I looked through my fringe, without moving my head, and saw the hot pink drink bottle sitting in the middle of his desk, in amongst piles of papers and a photo of his wife and two sons. I'd had a crush on his youngest son, Patrick, since I was eight years old—until he moved away to go to university. I swallowed hard. What would Mr Dean and his family think of me now?

The silence in the room was making noise in my head. Every muscle was restricted to the point where even if I wanted to run from the room, I didn't think my legs would carry me. Perhaps Mr Dean had cast a spell on me, making it impossible for my legs to move. His office was filled with wall-to-wall shelves of old books that absorbed the light. Perhaps I should just tell the truth. Perhaps that would be easier.

My mind would not be quiet as I waited for Mr Dean to begin the interrogation. Options seemed to run in, slap me, and then tag another idea to taunt me. If I told the truth, Paige would be expelled for sure. Then it would only be me and Keira at school, and that's if Keira would still be my friend after dobbing in Paige—*unlikely*. And then there was Megan. As much as I didn't want her to leave, I didn't want to be the reason that she had to stay here. She'd hate me. *Everyone would hate me.* No one would want to be friends with a dobber who'd gotten one friend expelled and another kicked out of her private school before she'd even had her first day.

It wasn't fair. This wasn't my fault. I hadn't wanted to drink the stuff. I'd only had a tiny sip, less than what the other girls had.

'Kat.' Mr Dean's voice was deep and calm. 'Do you want to tell me why Mr Wally sent you to my office?'

I shrugged. *Remember the plan, Kat. Stick to the plan.* I wiped my nose and steadied my breathing.

'You don't have any idea?'

I lifted my eyes slightly and pointed to the hot pink drink bottle.

'This is yours?' Mr Dean asked.

I nodded and swallowed hard. First lie to my principal.

'This pink drink bottle sitting on my desk here is yours?' I could sense Mr Dean trying to look into my face, to make eye contact. There was no way I was looking up into his face.

I nodded again.

'And the contents of the bottle that Mr Wally saw you drinking from-that is yours too?'

I paused for a moment. 'He didn't see me drinking it. He just saw me holding it.'

Through my fringe, I watched Mr Dean run his hand through his hair and sigh. He was pretty young for a principal.

He had a few wrinkles around his eyes, which kind of scrunched up when he smiled. It was a kind smile. I hated lying to him.

'What was in the bottle, Kat? The one Mr Wally took from you.'

'A chocolate milkshake.'

'Is that right?' He stood up and came around my side of his desk. He half leaned, half sat on the edge. 'Did you bring the contents of the bottle to school?' Silence. Just my breaths: short, shallow. 'Did you bring the bottle to school full, or did someone else fill it up, or add something to it, once you got here?'

I shook my head, but immediately regretted it. 'I mean, yes. I brought what was in it to school.' This lying thing didn't come naturally to me. 'It's my bottle and I brought the al—' I gulped. 'The chocolate milkshake to school to drink at lunch.'

'It's okay. We know there is alcohol in the bottle, Kat. That's why you're here. If it were just a chocolate milkshake, do you think you would be sitting here in my office having this chat with me?'

I shook my head and looked back down at the floor.

'What did you put in the milk? What alcohol is it?'

I shrugged. I had no idea.

'Kat, clearly the other girls have been chewing peppermint gum or something between when Mr Wally sat you out the front of my office and now. They're covering their tracks, but you're not. Why is that?'

I shrugged. 'I don't know anything about that. I think Keira might have had an Aero bar at recess; maybe they were sharing it and that's what you smelled?' I smiled on the inside—that was a good response. Perhaps I wasn't so bad at this lying thing after all.

'Look, Kat, I'm going to be straight with you.' Mr Dean lowered his voice. 'I spoke to Mrs Anderson before you came in and we have a theory I want to run by you, okay?'

I nodded and looked up into his face for a brief moment. His eyes looked desperate. I tucked my chin down against my chest.

'I think this is Paige's bottle that she brought to school containing alcohol for you all to try. But Mr Wally caught you with the bottle after everyone else had had a drink. Is that what happened?'

I shook my head. I wasn't lying. I had drunk some too. He'd left that part out. 'No, Mr Dean, it is my bottle.' I took a deep breath and held it.

I began the trail of lies that I had been told to tell. 'It's my drink. I brought it to school and had it with my lunch. None of the other girls had any. They don't even know why they're sitting outside the office.' I crossed my arms, looking past him to the window that revealed clear blue sky outside. 'They said something about Mrs Anderson organising for us to be sent to the office so she could prepare a surprise farewell for Megan.'

Mr Dean leaned back on his desk, staring at me with his big brown eyes. I refused to look into them. 'Kat, you realise I won't be able to protect you from this. There are going to be consequences. It is extremely serious.'

'It's all true, Mr Dean,' I said, my eyes fixed on his right shoe—he was wearing white socks under his black trousers. *Focus. End this. Finish the lie.* 'The girls out there don't know anything. I brought the drink to school. I've been stressing about Megan leaving school and Dad having another heart attack, and I found the drink in the back of our pantry and for some reason, I tried it. And it makes me feel better. I just wanted to get through Megan's last day. That's all. No one else even knew what I was doing.'

And there we had it. In one short meeting with the school principal, I'd gone from being an honest teenager who had hardly told a lie in her life, to being a downright expert on it.

Mr Dean sent me out to the wooden bench and I watched my three friends, one by one, walk into his office. They all confirmed my story: they didn't know why they were there, they didn't know what had been in my drink bottle. The lie was completed. By the end of the day, I'd have a school record—a reputation.

But at least I would have my friends there to support me through it all.

***

I spent the entire school day sitting on the bench, alone. My friends didn't come to visit me at lunch time. The only people I saw were teachers. And my parents.

Mum walked out of Mr Dean's office, her eyes puffy and red. She didn't say anything to me. She hardly even looked at me. She was dragging my little brother, George, around after her, pulling him in the direction of the toilets. It was something I hadn't considered, that in lying to Mr Dean, I would also have to lie to my parents. My heart filled with remorse, so much so that I contemplated running back into Mr Dean's office and blurting out the truth: *It wasn't me! It wasn't my drink bottle! I'd only had a tiny drink.*

It wasn't long before both my parents were standing in front of me. George was pretending to make his Batman toy fly around behind them. *The innocence of a four-year-old.*

'Hey.' Dad bent down in front of me. I smiled weakly and wiped the tears that were spilling over and running freely down my cheeks. You'd think I'd have run out of tears, I'd cried that much already. But, like Mum said to me when Dad was hooked up to all those machines in Intensive Care, tears are like love—just when you think you've cried all you can, you find a new, deeper level to cry from. 'What's going on with you?'

I gulped. Lying to my dad—okay. Here goes.

'I got into trouble.'

Dad nodded.

'I got caught with some alcohol.'

‘So I heard. You know, Mum said we don’t even own a drink bottle like that.’

I shrugged. ‘I bought it. I usually keep it on my desk at school.’ I gritted my teeth. Any of my teachers would be able to confirm that was a lie. I needed to keep calm, think things over before talking.

‘And the alcohol?’ Dad said. ‘Where’d it come from?’

I shrugged.

‘Mr Dean said you got it from our pantry.’

I looked at Mum, who was refusing to look at me. ‘Yeah, I found it up the back where the cooking stuff is.’ A lie. A big fat one. Surely they’d know I was lying about that too. This was too hard! There were too many holes in the story.

‘Honey, Mum doesn’t keep alcohol in the pantry. She doesn’t keep any in the house.’

‘It was really old,’ I panicked. ‘It must have been Grandpa’s, from when he was here once.’

Dad shook his head. ‘Why are you doing this, Kat? There are going to be some really big consequences for this. If you are covering for Pai— ... for any of your friends, you need to say so now. We’ve always told you to tell the truth, no matter what the consequences might be. You don’t always know what is going to happen to others involved. Telling the truth is always the best option.’

I lowered my head and stifled a sob. ‘I can’t, Dad.’

‘So, you’re going to stand by everything you have said to Mr Dean? To me, just now?’

I nodded.

Dad stood up and walked over to Mum. Her face was cold and unresponsive. I was crying so much that my snot and my tears were mixing into one steady stream of wetness that now covered most of my face. No sleeve was long enough for this level of sadness.

Mum came over. 'Clean your face up. Mr Dean wants to talk to us all in a minute.'

George looked at me and smiled as he watched Mum hand me his wet wipes.

I did what she said.

Mr Dean came out and beckoned Mum and Dad into his office. I shuffled along behind them and stood at the back of the room, watching George play at Mum's feet while they discussed my fate. Yes, there was talk about expulsion. But Mr Dean said, although it was a crime worthy of immediate expulsion, he wasn't going to enforce that this time, given that I'd never so much as had a detention in all my years of schooling. I sighed. Paige had been right; they weren't going to be as hard on me as they would have been on her.

The consequences were discussed as though I were a mere painting on a wall—invisible, faceless.

From Mum: grounding, other than church activities. I could cope with that.

From Dad: no sitting with my friends in any of our shared classes for the rest of the term.

My mouth fell open. I couldn't believe I'd been side-swiped by my own father.

Then came the big announcement from Mr Dean: 'We need to have a clear school-based consequence to show this behavior is not acceptable to all students in the school. I don't think I need to remind you that this situation needs to be taken extremely seriously.' Mr Dean placed his clasped hands on the desk in front of him. 'I cannot risk this sort of thing happening again by you, Kathleen, or any other student who might see you as getting off lightly.'

I bit my lower lip and held my breath.

'Our detention room runs at second lunch every day except Fridays,' Mr Dean said, watching me out of the corner of his eye. 'I suggest Kat be placed in these detention classes for the rest of the term.'

'What? Four days a week?' My hands slapped against my face as my mouth refused to close. Three faces glared back at me.

'Perfect,' Mum said, not taking her eyes off me.

Dad nodded. 'I think it's a good idea, too.'

Mr Dean's eyes lingered on the hot pink drink bottle sitting on his desk and nodded. 'She can start tomorrow.'

***

My sister, Rebecca, met me on the way to the car. She was suddenly there, walking beside me, her pace matching mine. She didn't look at me. Her senior school tie blew in the breeze as she walked and she held her straw hat down with her left hand. 'Is it true?' she asked.

'What?'

She made a *tsk* noise with her tongue. 'As if you don't know. The alcohol thing. What else would I be talking about?'

'How do you know about it?' The senior campus was right next door, but senior and middle school students weren't allowed to mix, except for before and after school.

'It's all over school,' Rebecca said. 'The pastor's daughter who's gone off.'

I stopped. 'What?'

Rebecca kept walking and I had to run a little to catch up.

'Who told you?'

Rebecca shrugged. 'People. Everyone knows.' She looked at me. 'Did you do it?'

I shook my head. 'I can't believe it.'

'So, you didn't do it?'

'Well, I've got the rest of the term in detention, I'm grounded and I'm not allowed to sit with my friends in class anymore.

Does it sound like I didn't do it?'

'You're an idiot,' Rebecca said. 'Seriously.'

Before I had the chance to explode at my crank of a sister, we were at the car park and Paige, Keira and Megan were standing near the gate. As I approached, Paige put her head down, while Keira looked out onto the road as though she hadn't seen me. Only Megan locked eyes with me. She smiled a sad smile and mouthed, 'You okay?' I nodded and turned to follow my parents to our car.

It only occurred to me once we were driving off that Megan had been walking out of Central High for the final time. I hadn't even given her a hug goodbye.

CHAPTER 4

I dreaded waking up the next morning, knowing I had to face a new day at school. A school without Megan *and* with lunchtime detention. I'd gone to sleep the night before with wet hair, without my doona pulled up around my face like I normally would in winter. Queensland winter nights could have some bite, but not enough to deliver the head cold I'd been hoping for. Instead, I woke up in the middle of the night with icy feet that made my legs ache.

I dragged myself around the house, wishing the morning had not really arrived. I wished I'd slept through the six weeks of detention and instead woken up at the beginning of the school holidays. An unexplained, sudden coma—that would be awesome. Or perhaps I'd somehow contract a paralysing syndrome where the best chance of recovery meant being put into a deep sleep for exactly six weeks—maybe a syndrome brought on by excessive lying.

As Mum pulled the car into the school parking lot, there were no friends there to meet me. No Megan. I couldn't stop my lip from quivering. I turned to smile at Mum, but my heart wasn't in it. She placed her hand on my upper arm. 'You'll be right. Have a good day.' She didn't kiss me goodbye this time. George smiled and manoeuvred his Batman toy to wave at me.

‘Try not to do anything too stupid today, will you,’ Rebecca said as she walked off towards the senior campus. I watched her, trying to picture myself walking that same path next year. My breakfast danced in my stomach. Without Megan here beside me, school was even more depressing than before, and the change to senior school brought no promise of relief.

I headed toward my homeroom. Other kids were standing around me, but I was completely alone. I was invisible. Everyone and no one watched me.

Keira turned and gave me a little wave and smile as Mrs Anderson let everyone into the classroom. Mrs Anderson pointed to a desk up the very back of the room. ‘Kat, that will be your seat for the rest of the term in English and any other classes you have in this room.’ That was most of my classes.

‘What?’ It came out so much louder than I had intended. ‘That’s not fair. Why?’

‘Because I said so, Kat. And that kind of attitude is not going to get you sitting back with your friends any faster.’

I looked at the desk right next to the corridor window; now everyone who walked by would see me sitting up the back of the classroom on my own. Friendless.

I was doomed to be stuck in a Groundhog-Day-type cycle of teachers coming and going, trapped in the same seat, next to the same window. At normal secondary schools, you changed classrooms practically every lesson. But no, Central had to be a ‘leader in new ideas and educational philosophy’, or so they kept telling us. Keira reckoned it was all propaganda.

But the class following English really stepped up the horridness of my day. It was math, which I used to kind of like when Megan was here. The advanced math group was smaller than the other classes, and the teacher let Megan and I work through the questions together. But now, I had no friend in the class. And to make it worse, when the boy in the hoodie walked into the room, he headed straight to the desk I was sitting at, and stood in front of it, staring at me.

'Are you right?' I asked.

'You're in my seat,' he said. He held a pencil and a black sketchbook in his hand. His eyes were sunken and dark, and some of his fridge hung down over the left side of his face.

'What?'

'That's my desk. Where I sit.'

I studied the quickest pathway to the door. 'Well, according to the fabulous teachers at Central, this is my desk now.' The boy held up his pencil, twirling it in his fingers as though he wanted to make a point of how sharp it was. I swallowed hard. 'Look, I have to sit here, alright?'

The boy slumped his shoulders and shook his head. He sat at the desk beside me and opened his sketchbook; only an empty metre of air separated our desks. Keira's stories of Mafia and murders ran through my mind when I looked down at his sketchbook. It was opened to a charcoal woman with big, frightened eyes. He drew the outline of a dagger in her hand, held up to her chest, then licked his pencil before thickening the dagger's blade.

I watched him out of the corner of my eye as the teacher droned on up the front. Eventually, he stopped drawing and stared at the wall, his hands twitching like he was in some kind of trance. At one point, he was so out of it, he didn't notice two boys throw spit-balls at him from behind their books. It was as though he didn't care that other kids were laughing at him.

When the boys eventually gave up on throwing things at him, the boy in the hoodie turned and looked at me. His dark eyes were dull and sad. I quickly looked away, hoping any possible family ties with the Mafia were no longer current.

***

I hugged my pencil case to my chest as I stood outside the door condemned with the 'Detention' sign. It opened onto a room with a storm-filled sky, void of any bright colours. A Year Eleven guy turned the lights on to reveal walls filled with anti-bullying posters and quotes about how life is better when you are kind to others and obey your parents and teachers. I groaned.

The detention teacher was Mr Wally.

'Ah, Kat,' he said, turning and looking me over. 'Welcome to detention. We have a special desk for you right over here'. He pointed to one of three desks sitting in the front corner of the room. 'We've made a special section just for students in long-term detention.'

I sighed and threw my pencil case on the table. Mr Wally frowned, before instructing the other students in the room to sit away from me.

I was pondering how I could be the only girl in the room when the boy in the hoodie walked in. After his finger-raising incident the previous day, and the way he had just drawn that woman with the dagger in his sketchbook, I shouldn't have been surprised that he was in detention as well. He was probably a permanent guest here.

He walked up to Mr Wally and they spoke quietly for a moment before he came and took a seat in my corner, his overly-sharpened pencil once again in his hand. As always, his hoodie was pulled up over his head. He sat down and picked up where he left off in math class—staring off into space.

I filled out the stupid worksheet that, apparently, you had to complete every time you were in detention. It was true or false questions about the school rules. One of the boys, a regular attender, asked if he could just photocopy the last one he'd filled out.

'No, Mr Johnston, you cannot,' Mr Wally said. 'You all must

fill this out and if you don't do it properly, I will make you come back tomorrow and do it again.' He glanced at me as he said it.

Once finished, I sat with my head on the desk, trying to ignore the fact that the boy in the hoodie was watching me. When I eventually turned to make eye contact with him, I groaned, willing him to leave me alone.

The boy chuckled.

'What?' I asked, raising my head. 'Is my pain entertaining you?'

The boy just raised his eyebrows and went back to his drawing.

'You have the social skills of a sloth,' I said.

He didn't look up. 'I didn't realise sloths had such terrible social skills.'

I screwed up my face and shook my head. 'Well, they're lazy and smelly and keep to themselves. Hardly friend-making material.'

He drew thick black lines across his paper, right through the middle of his drawing. 'Really? No one's even told me I smell before.'

In an attempt to pass the time and take my mind off the creepy boy in the hoodie, I evil-eyed Mr Wally as much as I could without getting caught. I imagined his face in a newspaper and drew a squiggly moustache, vampire teeth and big thick-rimmed glasses over his eyes. I left off the eyebrows, as he already had bushy ones that almost joined in the middle. When I added black lipstick to the mental image, he was goth personified. My revenge was sweet, even if I were the only one who knew about it.

I reread what I'd written on the worksheet twenty times. I'd decided to write Mr Dean an essay on the back, detailing the importance of having a good attitude towards school and how I needed to be working alongside my teachers, not against them. I coloured in all the 'o's and made flowers out of the 'g's.

I explained how sorry I was for my crimes, and how this one detention was all I needed to ensure I never did anything so stupid again. I contemplated expressing my feelings about what a horrible school Central was, but decided that wouldn't increase my chances of getting out of jail—detention—early.

My first detention was a long, boring forty minutes in purgatory, but I'd survived it. And it meant I only had 23 detentions left to sit through.

CHAPTER 5

Classes passed by like stations on an express train as I sat at my desk of banishment. The boy in the hoodie was my only company in math class, while in all my other classes I was forced to sit on my own. He only ever had his black sketchbook, a pencil sharpener, and a pencil on his desk. Nothing else. Never a math book—I don't even think he owned one. I'd often catch him staring in my direction, but not at me; he'd be looking through me to somewhere else. Or he'd have his eyes closed, as though he were sleeping, but still sitting upright in his chair.

I spent my time in detention filling in the stupid worksheets and counting the hundreds of ways my life currently sucked.

At home, things were just as depressing as they were at school. Mum was ignoring me; half the time she wouldn't even look at me. I was pretty convinced that she didn't love me anymore. Rebecca hassled me about my 'new-found life of crime' at every opportunity. And Dad only spoke to me when he really had to, which wasn't all that often. I didn't think it was fair they were treating me this way, since I hadn't really done anything wrong, other than tell some lies. But I guessed the problem was Mum and Dad didn't know that. I spent my days in my bedroom with my headphones on, doing everything I could to blot out the world and every thought of the boy in the hoodie.

At school, the more I sat near him, the more he got underneath my skin. I was yet to see him fill out one of the useless anti-bullying sheets in detention, and he never did any work in math. It was like there was a separate law, a separate set of rules for the boy in the hoodie. During Thursday's detention, I caught him watching me and threw him a fake smile in return. It made him laugh. I rolled my eyes.

'You don't think much of me, do you?' he said.

I shrugged and shook my head—but with such tiny movement, I wondered if he'd noticed.

'You know, it wouldn't kill you to smile every now and then. That wasn't a great smile you just gave me, but it was better than the scowl you usually wear.'

'Like you can talk.'

He smiled, but not enough to show his teeth. I couldn't tell if it was because he thought what I said was amusing, or true.

'Not everyone enjoys being locked up in this room, you know. Not everyone likes to be watched by boys they hardly know.'

He bobbed his head from side to side. 'There are worse places you could be.'

'Oh really?' I said. 'I can't think of any.'

The boy didn't reply. He turned a page in his sketchbook and started a new drawing.

'What are you drawing all the time, anyway?'

'Just whatever is in my head,' he said.

He filled in every bit of those sheets of paper, never leaving white space. 'You must have a busy head.'

'You don't?' He looked at me, into my eyes, as though he were trying to read my soul.

I looked away. 'No. I don't think I do.' My heart rate quickened and a strange sort of heat burned in my chest. I screwed up my nose. Stupid boy.

My head began to spin as it filled with the overwhelming sense of having had enough of detention, home, life and boys in hoodies! I was beginning to crack, I could feel it.

***

The weekend was upon me but I didn't know what was worse—coming to school where I spent my days with my heart in my feet, or having to stay at home, where I'd be invisible.

Around the house, Mum was still only speaking to me when she had to. Dad was being a bit better, but I could still feel the tension. Rebecca had gone back to the way things had been prior to my becoming the great disappointment—ignoring me.

I spent the weekend curled up in bed with my headphones on, reading the best parts of my favourite books over and over. I reread *The Maze Runner*, which I loved all the more, because this time I could identify with the characters—the feeling of entrapment, hopelessness, fear for the future. I finally understood the draw that Thomas had to the Maze and his need to be a runner. I needed to be a runner. I didn't care about the consequences, I needed to escape from my life before I imploded.

As I lay on my bed, tears rolling down my cheeks, George wandered into my room. He climbed into my bed and snuggled under my arm as I stroked his little four-year-old head. To him, nothing had changed. He still loved me just like he did before the lie. He'd still come into my room and beg me to put my headphones on him, and then he'd wag his bottom around in time to my music. He'd still take my hand and beg to be lifted for a cuddle. His eyes would still light up when I walked into a room. I longed for George's innocence, and how easily he made everything okay again.

I barely made it out of the house for church, and didn't speak to anyone the whole time I was there. I refused to play 'happy family' this weekend, no matter how much my father pleaded with me.

To make things worse, when school rolled around again on Monday morning, something was up with Paige, but I couldn't figure out what. The previous week, I'd watched from a distance as she rode a crazy mood roller-coaster. She would say hello with a smile one morning, then give me daggers from her seat during class. She burst into tears when Mrs Anderson called on her to answer a question on *The Hobbit* one morning, but then got angry later that day in history about how no one ever picked her to answer questions.

But this Monday morning was worse. I watched from the back of the classroom as Paige sat with red, puffy eyes and a shiny jumper sleeve, refusing to do any work in English. I tried a number of times to get her attention but she never looked back at my table. So, when I noticed Keira was up the front sharpening her pencil, I broke my lead on purpose and joined her by the bin.

'What's with Paige?' I whispered.

'Something bad happened over the weekend.' Keira spun her pencil around in the sharpener even though it was already sharp. 'She wouldn't give details, just said her mum was gone and this time she wouldn't be coming back. Something about her step-dad getting caught in the act, but I don't know. She was pretty upset before school.'

'Wow. Her mum left without her? That's crazy.'

'Yeah, like, she was crying and everything when I found her in the tunnel behind the sports shed before school. I've never seen her like that before.'

Mrs Anderson cleared her throat loudly and when I turned to look at her, she was frowning at us. I smiled sweetly and held my sharpened pencil up for her to see, before heading back to my seat. There was no way I could concentrate on the history quiz in front of me. I looked over to where Paige sat, staring out the classroom window. I wondered what had gone on in her house, knowing that she'd never really got along with her step-dad. Things must have been bad for her mum to have left and not taken Paige with her.

Just as the bell rang for recess, Mrs Anderson stopped the exiting class and looked directly at me. 'Kat, stay back, please.' I stopped myself from rolling my eyes and sat in one of the chairs closest to the door as everyone escaped into the corridor. 'I won't hold you up. I know you have detention again today.'

'Thanks,' I said, trying to keep the sarcasm out of my voice. I desperately wanted to get away so I could talk to Paige.

Mrs Anderson sat in the chair beside me and paused for a moment. If she hadn't wanted to hold me up, this wasn't a great start. 'Mr Dean and your parents wanted me to remind you that you need to be making the right decisions on how you spend your time outside of your classes.'

'You mean *the people* I spend my time with?' I couldn't believe she was taking up my free time to lecture me. 'I'm lucky to get twenty minutes of break time a day, thanks to these detentions, and you're telling me not to spend it with my friends?'

'I only want to see you reaching your full potential.'

'You want me to spend my school days locked inside and friendless, you mean.'

Mrs Anderson raised one eyebrow. 'No, that's not it at all. We just want you to be making good choices. In friends, in activities, in your decision-making.'

'What does everyone have against Paige?' I said, trying not to sound angry. 'You all have it in for her. But she's been my friend since primary school and she's been through a lot. You all should just give her a break. You should give us all a break.' I stood up. 'Is that all?' My heart was racing. I'd never spoken to a teacher like that before. My knees were going to collapse from under me if I didn't get out of that room.

Mrs Anderson nodded, a sad look on her face. I almost felt sorry for her. Perhaps I shouldn't have yelled at her. But seriously, who did she think she was? I hated this school. I hated Mr Dean and Mrs Anderson and all the teachers who were making my life miserable.

As I burst out of the school building, the sun's brightness hurt my eyes; even in winter, the Queensland sky was often cloudless. Every student in the school must have been standing in the courtyard, trying to catch some of the warm rays.

By the time I found Paige and Keira, the bell was about to ring. They were standing with three Year Eleven boys. Paige was flashing flirtatious smiles and laughing with the three boys, all of them with their eyes fixed on her. But she went quiet as soon as I arrived. One of the boys noticed me standing on the outside of the group and suggested it was time for them to leave.

'What are they doing here on our campus?' I asked, as the boys headed back towards the senior campus. 'They're not supposed to be over here during school hours.'

Paige rolled her eyes. 'Whatevs, Mary.'

Paige and Keira chatted all the way to the art room. I walked a little too close to Keira, trying to listen in on the conversation. 'I've been called to Principal Dean's office twice already today,' Paige said. My heart sank, fearful Mr Dean still thought Paige was behind the pink drink bottle episode. I dropped behind, unable to stand hearing about Paige lying to the principal any more than I could handle thinking about the lies I'd told him.

At lunchtime, I headed to the detention room with a head full of Paige and a million questions. I was trapped in a world of windowless walls, and rules that seemed unfair and completely unnecessary. The worst bit: it was only week two of detention. If my parents had let me have Facebook, then I might have been able to communicate with Paige or even Keira more. But I wasn't allowed to use Messenger, let alone social media, until I was sixteen. And that felt like it was forever away.

In math that afternoon, I watched the boy in the hoodie drawing. Although bizarre, watching him draw was somewhat intoxicating. Sometimes his drawings were really dark; people with black faces and wild hair, with strange markings on their bodies and ripped clothing. He'd draw dark buildings in the background and burnt out trees that had no life left in them. Never a smile. Never a flower, or even a leaf. It resonated with something inside me, how sometimes in life it was impossible to find colour—but maybe there was beauty in the grey.

The next day, the detention room was musty and smelled of teenage boy. The boy in the hoodie walked into detention, late again. I tried my best to ignore him. *Who gets to walk into detention late without so much as a word to the teacher?* When the boy in the hoodie sat down at his seat near me, I frowned at him. He didn't take notice of me.

'You're late,' I said.

He shrugged and took a pencil out of his pocket. It wasn't fair that the rules didn't apply to him. Who was he and what made him so special that the teachers treated him differently to everyone else?

'What did you do to be here in detention, anyway?' I blurted out, anger sitting on the sidelines, waiting to jump in. 'It must have been pretty bad to be here every day, like me.'

He raised his eyebrows at me, and then shrugged. 'Just stuff.'

I watched him drawing. He was shading the background grey, while adding trees with giant claws for branches.

'Your drawings are so dark. Why don't you put colour in them?'

'How do you know I don't?'

'Well, I'm yet to see it if you do.'

'I don't need colour to express what I'm drawing.'

I could so identify with that. I placed my head down on my desk. 'Why won't you tell me what you did to get into detention? I've never seen you get into any trouble with the teachers and they don't seem to care if you hand in work or not.'

'So?'

'So, it's not fair. I don't see why the rules should be different for you. You are a mystery.' Was that a smirk I saw under his hoodie? 'I want to know why the teachers treat you different.'

'I don't see what it has to do with you.'

I let out a deep sigh. 'I just want to know. Everyone at this school has it in for me, since I ... well, you don't want to know what I did to be here,' I said, looking at my nails and pretending to clean them, while still watching the boy in the hoodie out of the corner of my eye. He must have known I was watching him. He looked at me for the briefest moment before picking up his pencil sharpener and sharpening his pencil—right there at his desk. Mrs Kelly was the teacher on detention duty and she hated pencil sharpenings anywhere but in the bin. Everyone knew you were supposed to go to the bin, especially in her classes. It made me smile, like it was a kind of silent protest about the stupid rules they make up in schools. It was another act of defiance, even though the rules didn't seem to apply to him anyway.

I'd almost forgotten the boy in the hoodie and I were talking. When he spoke, it made me jump a little. His voice was deep. 'It is conceivable that I already know why you are in detention.'

I frowned. I couldn't see how he could possibly know, when he never spoke to anyone. The boy in the hoodie turned his pencil around with his fingers, smoothing out the point. Then, without looking at me, he said, 'It's my birthday today.'

I turned up my nose a little. 'How old are you?'

He closed his eyes and a little sigh left his lips. 'Sixteen.'

'Sixteen? But you're only in Year Nine. I don't even turn fifteen until the end of term.'

He shrugged. 'Yeah, well, life is messed up sometimes.'

I took a piece of chicken out of my lunch box and began picking the meat off it. 'Why did you tell me that?' I asked.

'I thought someone should know.' He went back to his drawing, a pile of pencil sharpenings in a little pyramid on his desk.

I leaned over and blew hard so they floated off his desk and scattered across the floor. 'Well, Happy Birthday then,' I said and smiled a little.

He smiled back at me, wide and goofy, with all his teeth showing. And I found myself thinking it was the nicest thing anyone had done to me all week.

CHAPTER 6

I lay in bed, my orange doona with big blue and purple stripes bringing me no comfort. Tonight, it looked dull and childish. Every time I closed my eyes, I was one of those pieces of pencil clippings sitting on the boy in the hoodie's desk. I was small, insignificant. And someone was blowing on me, sweeping me off the edge of the desk so I was falling, slowly at first. But then the floor came racing towards me, rushing at me and with just seconds to spare, I'd open my eyes, only to see my fish tank light casting freaky shadows around the bedroom.

I wanted to get my family, school, detention, and the boy in the hoodie as far out of my mind as possible. But I'd failed to find a book worth reading in the library during the week and my phone was flat so I couldn't listen to music—Rebecca and I shared a charger and there was no way I was going to go knocking on her door to get it. She'd been really rude and moody after school. And since Mum and Dad had a 'no TV on school nights' rule, I'd been left with only my inner thoughts to listen to.

I looked at my fingernails; they were a decent length, but not very sharp. I wrapped my hand around my wrist and squeezed it hard, manoeuvring my fingers so the nails began to dig into the skin. I could see the dints forming on my arm. The discomfort felt good, real, and took my mind off the deeper pain that was clouding my mind. I undid my watch and positioned my hand further up my wrist. Oh, the markings left were even better there, the pain more intense. I squeezed until tears began to form under my eyelids, my heart thumping in my chest.

The sound of my bedroom door opening snapped me back. I threw my left hand under my doona and sat up straight. Dad walked in.

'You in bed already, honey?'

I nodded, then let out a squeaky, 'Yep.'

He came and sat on my bed. 'You doing okay?'

'Not really,' I said, fighting to keep my emotions under control. I rubbed my stinging wrist. What was I doing?

'Tough couple of weeks, huh?'

I nodded. It was no use. Tears spilt down my face.

'So, tell me, what's the worst thing at the moment?' Dad asked.

I shrugged. 'Everything.'

Dad shot me a pity smile. 'More specific?'

I considered the question; there were so many things. Not sitting with my friends in class. Being grounded. Megan not at Central anymore. Detention—though, detention was not as bad as it first had been. There was something about being in detention with the boy in the hoodie that was starting to make it a bit more bearable. Something about him that was starting to make me smile when I thought about him. Detention may have been ruining my social life, but it was no longer the worst thing I had to deal with. In the end, I answered, 'I think it's probably Mum.'

'Oh?'

I pulled one of my teddies hard into my chest and tried to swallow. 'She's hardly talked to me since that day at school. She hardly looks at me.' I bit my bottom lip. 'I don't think she loves me anymore.'

Dad sighed. 'Kat, this has been difficult for your mum, too. Don't try to judge how she feels about you. That's not fair on your mum. She loves you. That's why she's taking this hurt so badly. But she'll get over it.'

'I didn't mean to hurt her.'

'We know that. Sometimes, when something like this happens, children'—I cringed at the word—'can't see, they can't predict how it's going to affect other people. That's why we want to make sure you're telling us the truth. Because this has hurt your mum so much.'

'I don't see why. I'm the one having to go to detention every day and not see my friends.'

'Well, for one thing, we know you're lying about where you got the alcohol. Alcohol can be a dangerous thing for some people. It was a dangerous thing for Grandpa Irving—so much so, he died from having too much. When he passed away, your mum made the decision not to keep any alcohol in the house, even for cooking. She went through the cupboards and threw it all out.'

'Oh.' I knew Mum didn't like alcohol, but I didn't know why.

'Plus, since your grandfather died, your mum has been really outspoken about the effect of alcohol on families. Haven't you noticed how she's always posting stuff on Facebook about it?'

I shrugged. 'I'm not allowed Facebook yet, remember?'

'Oh yeah. Well, it really hurt your mum, not only that you took alcohol to school, but that you said you got it from her pantry. We know you're lying about that and we are disappointed that you won't tell us the truth.'

I ran my hand along my wrist. Man, it still stung. Why did consequences have to go on for so long, and continue to hurt so much?

'It will take a little bit for Mum to stop being hurt by this,

Kat. She still loves you, but it has really hurt and embarrassed her. We never thought you would do something like this. We always considered you to be the sensible one, between you and your sister.'

Stab to my heart, a big long knife twisting and turning around inside my chest. 'Mum just needs time to process it.'

I nodded, unable to find breath to speak.

'So, tell me, why did you do it?'

'I wanted my friends to like me.' At least that wasn't a lie. 'I just want to fit in.'

'Can I say,' he sighed deeply, 'that is a pretty stupid reason to do something. You can't get much more foolish when it comes to an explanation for getting into this much trouble. Maybe you could think about that for a while.' He leaned over and kissed me on the forehead.

'Dad,' I caught his arm as he stood to go. 'Can I go to St Andrew's next year for senior school? With Megan?'

He looked at me with a furrowed brow. 'I don't think so. Their fees are really high.'

'I thought, you know, with Megan going there now that maybe there's people at that school I could be friends with. Friends you and Mum might like better.'

'It isn't your friends so much as your resolve to do the right thing that is the issue, Kat.' He narrowed his eyes. 'We're running a tight ship at the moment. I'm afraid that until George is school age, and Mum might go back to work, we don't have a lot of choice in terms of schools for you.'

'Can't the church give you a pay rise or something?'

'The church can hardly afford to pay me what they do now. One day, yes, we all hope that will be able to happen, but we've got a long road ahead of us before we can afford a pay rise for me.'

'I really want to change schools.' Tears trickled down my face again. 'I hate Central. I hate the teachers. I know I would be much happier at St Andrew's.'

'Well, like I said, in a couple of years we could look into it.'

'A couple of years? I'll be practically finished school by then.'

Dad nodded. 'I know, honey. I'm sorry.'

I shook my head. Asking to go to St Andrew's was never going to get me anywhere. Of course the answer would be no. I was doomed to being poor, friendless and living with a family that just didn't get me.

Dad held out Rebecca's iPad to me. 'Do you want to check your emails? See if there's one from Megan?'

I shook my head. 'No. I checked them earlier. There was an email from Megan, but I didn't read it.'

'Oh? Why not?'

'The subject line was, *Update: My new school is awesome.* I couldn't bring myself to open it.'

'Oh.' Dad swiped his finger across the iPad's screen. 'Well, how about you help me with planning our next holiday. Any ideas where you'd like to go?'

I rolled my eyes. So, we had money for family holidays, but not enough to send me to a private school?

Dad and his stupid plans for the world's most boring family holidays—they were always train trips. Dad was obsessed with trains and he didn't consider anything a holiday unless it required watching the world go by from a train carriage.

'Tasmania? I've always thought it sounded like a quaint place to visit.'

Dad frowned. 'You're teasing me. Come on, be serious.'

'Okay, well, what about Cairns?'

'The Sunlander. Oh yeah.' Dad sighed, a longing look in his eyes. 'That's up there on the bucket list. But we might need to hold off on that one until retirement—when we can afford it.' His mouth opened widely as he laughed. Not having any money, even to go on his beloved train trips, was just a joke to him. 'We might need to settle for the tilt train to Rocky, I reckon.'

'Rockhampton?' I groaned. Stupid city that had nothing going for it.

'We could see about going to the caves this trip, 'ey?'

I gave a weak smile. 'George would love that. The Batcave.'

Dad leaned in and kissed me. 'Good night, honey. Hope you sleep okay. Remember, you may feel like this term isn't going too good, but you can still end it well.'

His words were nothing but an empty cliché.

CHAPTER 7

When I woke up on Thursday morning, I immediately remembered it was another school day with another detention—but this time, my stomach didn't lurch into a pit of despair. In fact, I realised I was almost looking forward to it. *Almost.*

In detention, the boy in the hoodie once again sat down in the desk next to mine. Instead of picking up his pencil to start drawing, he sat looking at me, as though he was expecting me to say something. I raised my eyebrows. He smiled a little.

'Ah, how was your birthday yesterday?' I asked. Was that what he was expecting?

He tilted his head from side to side. 'I've had better. But, under the circumstances, it was okay.'

He pulled out a small tin of watercolour pencils. 'From my uncle,' he said, holding up the lipstick red one, before putting it back down to pick up his usual grey lead. 'It seems you're not the only one who's noticed the lack of colour in my artwork.'

'Nice,' I said, tilting my head. I narrowed my eyes and looked into the face of the boy in the hoodie. I wondered what circumstances he could have been talking about, and what he had done to land him in detention like me.

I looked up at the supervising teacher to find him buried

in a pile of paperwork. Usually the on-duty teacher would come armed with a coffee cup and newspaper, or marking—something equally as thrilling to do. One of the teachers last week had spent the whole time sleeping. But whichever way, they generally wouldn't say a word the whole lunch break.

'So, how is it you know already what I did to end up in detention?' I asked. The boy in the hoodie sat hunched over his piece of paper, his sharpened pencil making small, precise lines within the drawing. 'I can't see how you'd know,' I said, sitting up straight and flicking my ponytail over my shoulder. The detention room was quiet. There'd been a couple of days when it was just the two of us—hoodie boy and the alcoholic—in detention. But today there was one other boy in the room. He was short, even for a Year Seven kid, and looked so scared I don't think I saw him lift his head up from filling in his detention form the whole forty minutes.

'I don't *think* I know. I know.' The boy in the hoodie paused his pencil but didn't look up at me. 'You drank alcohol on school grounds.'

I raised my eyebrows. 'Pretty stupid, huh?'

The boy tilted his head from side to side. 'You could have done worse.'

I picked up the piece of paper on my desk and looked at the same words I'd already read fifteen times, but I kept watching him out of the corner of my eye. He was concentrating so hard on his drawing that I was sure I could have got up and performed as part of a flash mob and he wouldn't have noticed. His face had more colour today and his eyes had softened—not quite so dark—and I suspected he'd had a haircut, though it was difficult to tell under the hoodie.

'What's your name?' I asked before I could shut my mouth to stop the words escaping.

He stopped drawing. 'What's yours?' he asked, his eyes not leaving his drawing.

'Kat.'

'That's what everyone calls you, but that's not who you are. What's your full name?' His lips moved slightly as he began drawing again. His hair fell over one eye as he moved his pencil back and forth, shading what was beginning to look like a woman's face.

'Miss Kathleen Maree Morrow.' It was all I could do to stop myself from sliding under the table. I sounded ridiculous!

'Really?' The boy looked at me with amusement. 'Do you always give your full name like that?'

Heat rose from my heart up into my cheeks. 'No.'

He put his pencil down on the middle of the face he was shading. She had large eyes and the beginnings of long, flowing hair. She was stunning, but she looked disappointed, maybe even unhappy. Her eyes reminded me of my own, of how I had looked in the mirror over the past few weeks.

'Who are you drawing?'

'My mother,' he said, choosing a sky-blue pencil from his new tin.

'She is beautiful.'

'Yes, she is.'

'Do you live with her?'

The boy looked at me with a frown, but didn't answer my question. He started adding blue to the woman's eyes.

'You never told me what your name is.'

'My name'—he paused, as though deciding if he were going to tell me or not—'is Adrian. Adrian Jacobs.'

'Your name is Adrian?' My eyebrows shot up.

He looked at me out of the corner of his eyes, squinting a little. 'Yes, Miss Kathleen Maree Morrow, it has been my whole life.'

My heart skipped a beat as my name flowed from his lips like that. He made it sound beautiful, as though it were music. I mentally fought the heat rising to my cheeks. 'Adrian just seems a bit plain.'

'Plain?' he smiled a big, dopey grin. He seemed to be enjoying watching me squirm, asking stupid questions. 'What were you expecting?'

I rubbed my face with my hands and shook my head. 'I don't know. Maybe something…stronger? Something tougher. Like Fred or Eric.'

The boy in the hoodie—*Adrian*—laughed at me. 'Fred and Eric? They're the best tough names you could come up with?'

I shrugged, wishing I hadn't said anything.

I looked at the teacher at the front of the room, but he now had his head tilted up towards the ceiling with his mouth slightly ajar. I didn't know this teacher's name, but Adrian said he was a sleeper. He had a habit of starting off detention marking essays and ending up having a nap.

'I don't get it,' Adrian said. 'What's with Eric being a tough name?'

'Haven't you read *Divergent*?'

'I saw the movie.'

I rolled my eyes. 'The book was heaps better. Eric is the leader of Dauntless. He was even more horrible in the book than he was in the movie.'

'Yeah well, I didn't like *Divergent*. Most of those male characters were too much like people I knew.'

'That can't be true. They were pretty messed up characters.'

'Tell that to my brother.' Adrian looked straight at me. 'Peter—he's the one who reminds me of my brother.'

'It's only a story. It's not true,' I said.

Adrian didn't say anything.

I cleared my throat. 'Where is he now?'

'Who?'

'Your brother.'

Adrian shrugged. 'He left home last year. I woke up one morning and he was gone. I haven't heard from him since.'

I pretended to look at my worksheets, so I didn't have to think about what it would be like to have someone in your family just get up and leave one day. The detention form for the day was more of the same stuff: how to be a good friend; how to get involved in the community; the importance of being truthful; and my favourite, ten things you can do to show your parents you love them. Who even writes this stuff?

'So, what about Fred?' Adrian asked.

'Who's Fred?'

'Your other tough name.'

'Oh,' I laughed. 'I don't know. I think it sounds tough. It's short, to the point. There's no wondering how to spell a name like Fred. It is how it sounds. You hear each letter, they're in their order as they should be. Nothing to hide.'

'Is that what you think being strong and tough is about? Being up front and not hiding anything?'

'Yes, I do. Being tough is not being afraid of anything, even things within yourself.'

'That's not what tough is.' The boy looked thoughtfully at his pencil.

'Really?' I opened my lunch box and picked up a chicken leg. 'Then what is it?'

'Why do you eat chicken every day for lunch?'

I looked from the chicken leg and back to Adrian. I frowned. 'I don't eat sandwiches, if that's what you mean. I'm not allowed to eat stuff with gluten in it.'

'By choice or by diagnosis?'

'Diagnosis.'

'There was a kid at my last school who was gluten-free and he had to sit on his own at lunchtime, in case he got even a crumb on him from someone else's lunch.'

'Yeah, well, I'm only intolerant but the doctor said it could become more serious at any time. If I have gluten, it gives me horrible stomach cramps and makes me really tired and stuff.'

'Nasty.'

I finished eating as much chicken as I could without getting it all over my face. 'What is your definition of tough then, Fred?' I asked.

Adrian smiled and then put his head down for a moment. When he looked back up, he had a real serious look on his face. 'Being tough is staying and fighting, even when you're scared.' He picked up his pencil and toyed with the eraser at the end of it. 'But it's also about knowing when to leave, and leaving before it's too late. Being tough is living with the consequences of your actions. It's working through them, while not running away from what really matters.'

'Yeah, I know all about having to live with consequences,' I mumbled. Adrian looked at me, puzzlement on his face. His pencil hovered over the eye he was shading in. 'You must be very close to your mother to be able to draw her like that.'

Adrian cleared his throat. 'I don't live with my mother, Miss Kathleen Maree Morrow. Drawing her helps me remember what she looks like, how vulnerable she was—is—and the importance of protecting her.' He looked into my face, then his eyes went glazy. 'She didn't know how to be tough; she didn't understand what it meant to stay. She didn't know when to leave.' He went back to drawing his pictures. 'She needed me to be tough for her, I just didn't know it. But I get it now. I know how to be tough now.'

I ate the rest of my lunch in silence while Adrian concentrated on his drawing. I wondered about the boy in the hoodie's definition of tough. It was true; it was difficult to stay and follow through on the consequences of your actions. But I wasn't sure what he meant about the part where you also had to stay and not run away from what really mattered. The problem was, I wasn't totally sure what mattered in life. I was beginning to think things would be less complicated if I knew the things that really mattered to me. Then, I might know which things to fight for and which things to run away from. Then, perhaps I'd know when I needed to be tough.

***

That weekend, I awoke to the smell of pancakes. I breathed a slow sigh of relief—if Dad was cooking us pancakes, maybe things were starting to go back to the way they used to be. It made me determined to be as good as possible for the entire weekend.

Rebecca followed me into the kitchen and we sat side by side at the bench. She placed her head down, her hair a bird's nest resting on top of an empty plate, and let out a groan.

'Are you okay?' I asked, trying to sound pleasant.

Rebecca groaned again. 'George kept crying out during the night because he kept losing his Batman toy.' She gave me a look as though it were my fault. 'I must have gotten up for him at least three times last night.' Rebecca turned to Mum. 'Can't one of Kat's punishments be having George back in her room early?'

'You only have another two months to go, and then it will be Kat's turn again,' Mum said. 'Unless of course you two would rather go back to sharing a room?'

Both Rebecca and I shook our heads fiercely. We'd almost killed each other when we'd shared a room. We barely got along with each other now. Having George share my room for six months was a much better option than having to share all the time with Rebecca. *Especially* since it was her six months to have him.

Mum pulled the tea towel off Dad's freshly cooked stack of pancakes and lifted a couple onto each of our plates. I spread butter and raspberry jam over mine, though I didn't feel much like eating them. I used my fork to toy with them instead.

'Guilt is a great appetite suppressant,' Rebecca said as she downed her pancakes more quickly than George could empty his collection of Thomas the Tank Engine trains on the floor.

I scrunched my nose up at her.

'Guilt!' George repeated from the other side of the room. Mum smiled at him and congratulated him on using such a big word.

I took a mouthful and chewed it slowly in Rebecca's ear.

'You're gross.' She moved away from the bench.

Mum looked at me and chuckled—a definite change. In fact, I think Mum had even made eye contact with me a few times since I'd sat down at the bench for breakfast.

But, as it turned out, the smile had been nothing but an attempt to make me feel secure before delivering another kick in the gut.

'Kat, come and sit down on the couch with me,' Mum said. The juice I swigged in preparation didn't go down easy. 'I need to talk to you.'

Dad encouraged George down from the table and followed us to the couch. My mouth went dry. What was so serious that Dad was coming to talk to me, too?

'I spoke to Mrs Harold last night,' Mum said. Mrs Harold was Megan's mum. She's super nice. 'She told me Megan admitted to drinking some of the alcohol the other week at school too.'

I swallowed hard. 'What? No,' I said. 'There's no way she would have done that.'

Would she?

I hadn't checked my email since I'd got that one saying how great her new school was. Perhaps she'd tried.

'Well, Mrs Harold said Megan's story sounds pretty credible.'

I ran my hands through my hair. Now my parents and Mr Dean would both know that I'd at least lied about being the only one who had drunk the alcohol at school. I rubbed sweaty palms down my pajama pants. Mum and Dad sat looking at me, stupid looks of 'it's okay, honey, you can tell us the truth now' written all over their faces. I suddenly had a strong need for fresh air.

I couldn't understand why Megan had confessed to her mum. The lie had been going so well; there had been no need for Megan to admit her guilt! 'Is Megan still allowed to go to her new school?'

Mum nodded. 'Mrs Harold and Megan went to see Mr Dean, but he said that since Megan confessed after she had already left Central, he didn't feel it appropriate to pass the information on to her new school.' Mum looked at Dad as if she was talking to him as much as she was to me. 'I think he was being kind to Megan. He could have made things difficult for her, if he'd wanted.'

'I think,' Dad said, rubbing his forehead, 'Mr Dean knows there is more going on here than what you two girls are saying.'

I nodded slowly.

'I think Mr Dean knows that you two are making this story up. That you're protecting someone.'

'I did try the alcohol. I drank some, just like the others.' Blood was racing to my head. I had to keep the lie going—but how could I do that now?

'Others?'

'Megan.'

'And?'

'I can't tell you.' Tears spilt down my cheeks. I pulled my sleeve down over my hand and wiped my eyes. 'Even if there is more to the story, more that's going on, I can't tell you.'

'So—there is more?' Mum asked.

I shrugged.

George wandered into the room and threw himself into my lap, his Batman toy hitting me in the face as he climbed up. I held him close.

'Kathleen, you know,' Dad said, 'this story you're telling is more than just about you. It is a reflection on Mum, on me, and on our whole family. And because of that, it reflects badly on the church as well. I know that's not your fault, but it's the way the world works. This doesn't just put you in a bad light, that light shines out and hits all of us. Do you understand what I'm saying?'

'Yes and I'm really sorry.' I held George tight even though he was fighting to get down from my knee. 'I didn't mean to make you look bad. I truly didn't.' I turned to Mum. 'What Dad said about Grandpa and everything—I didn't think of that and I'm really, really sorry.'

Mum reached over and kissed me on the forehead.

'But, I can't tell you guys.' I looked across at Dad, pleading with him to understand. 'I can't tell you. Please, don't make me.'

'As Mr Dean said to me'—Dad brushed a stray hair from across my face—'you're a good kid who has made a bad decision. We believe that too. This is just what you've done, it's not who you have become. You're better than this. And we hope one day you'll be able to tell us the whole truth.'

I gritted my teeth.

'I don't want to go to Central anymore,' I said. 'I want a new start, to move somewhere else. I hate this town and all the people at my school.' I pulled George back further on my lap.

'Kat, running away isn't going to solve your problems, they'll just go with you,' Dad said. 'Making the right choices every day, that is what will make a difference in your life.'

Blah blah: nothing that I hadn't heard before. They didn't get it! They didn't understand me, or what was going on in my life. 'Is that all?' I stood up, but Dad gestured for me to sit back down. This wasn't over yet.

CHAPTER 8

'We're not done. We also need to talk about Paige.' Dad squirmed around in his seat, not really looking at me. Megan's confession wasn't doing me any favours so far.

'What else is there to say?' I said. 'You don't like Paige. I do. But my opinion doesn't count in this house, so I lose.'

'That's not true, Kat. You know we've always struggled with some of the friends you have chosen. But you are a good friend, a faithful friend, and that is admirable.'

I managed to restrain from rolling my eyes.

Mum leaned forward on her seat. 'What we're trying to say is we don't want you to have anything more to do with Paige.'

I looked at Mum. 'What do you mean?'

'I mean, we think she is a bad influence on you,' Mum said. 'We have been saying that for a long time now. We want you to take some ownership of the people you are choosing to spend time with. Now that Megan has left the school, it might be a good opportunity for you to find some new friends.'

I could have caught ping-pong balls in my mouth, my jaw dropped so low. Were they really banning me from seeing Paige?

'The thing is, Paige has started getting into trouble for life choices that we don't want you influenced into doing as well,' Dad said.

'I don't understand,' I tried to say in an angry voice, but my throat tightened and it came out squeaky. George laughed.

'Kat,' Mum said. 'We heard Paige has taken up smoking, for one thing. Mrs Anderson is convinced of it. And we know how much influence Paige has on you, how persuasive she can be.'

Muscles were tightening in my throat, causing a burning sensation, but I still opened my mouth to defend my friend. 'Don't you think—'

'Don't, Kat.' Dad put his hand up in front of me. I almost burst out laughing it was so ridiculous. 'We know she hasn't been officially caught yet, but Mrs Anderson said she's sure Paige is smoking after school. A couple of teachers saw her walking home with a lit cigarette in her hand. Heads of campus always find out these sorts of things, Kat.'

I stifled a chuckle. Mrs Anderson would like to think the teachers knew everything—but there was plenty of stuff going on at school Mrs Anderson knew nothing about.

'Mrs Anderson has received reports of Paige coming to school smelling of smoke and she thinks it won't be long before she starts bringing them to school. Mrs Anderson has been really worried about you. We all have. We're just glad you're in detention now so you won't get dragged into it too.'

Sarcasm came and joined me on the couch. I narrowed my eyes. 'You're glad I'm in detention, Dad?'

Dad shrugged. 'Of course we'd rather that this had never happened, but as far as I'm concerned, it's the silver lining in this whole thing.'

I wanted to cry and scream at the same time. I wish they'd just butt-out and leave me alone!

Mum placed her hand on mine. 'You have to admit, if Paige has started smoking, there's every chance Keira has too. Would you be able to say no? Especially now that Megan is not at Central?'

I knew Mum was right, but there was no way I was going to admit that. I drew my hand out from under Mum's and clasped them in my lap, my head down. I couldn't bear to look at mum or dad.

'There are some things going on in Paige's life,' Dad continued. 'Things that are causing her to react badly and we don't want you mixed up with that.'

'What—you mean her mum leaving?'

'There are lots of things going on,' Mum said. 'Things you don't need to know about. Things that we—'

'What are you talking about?' I yelled, the lump in my throat spilling out into a hundred words that I wanted to say but couldn't get my lips around. 'I know there's some bad things going on with Paige—that's why it's important that I see her! When someone is hurting, you don't take their friends away. She needs me. Keira and I are all she's got.'

Mum reached out her hand to try to take mine, but I yanked it away. I glared from one parent to the other. They both just looked at me, guilt on their faces.

'That's what you're doing, isn't it? The meeting with Principal Dean? All these punishments you came up with? They're all things that stop me from being with Paige. The detentions, the grounding, not being allowed to sit with my friends in class? I bet you're glad I took that alcohol to school, 'cause now you have a way of controlling me. It's not fair. It's not fair!'

'We're not trying to control you,' Dad said. 'We would rather you were friends with girls in your class who share the same values that we share as a family, not someone who is trying to get you involved in, well, some of the things that Paige is getting herself involved in.'

'We love that you want to support your friend at this difficult time in her life,' Mum said. 'But, the truth is, we don't think you're strong enough to be the good influence Paige needs. We think she'll just lead you even further astray.'

Mum looked at Dad and I saw him nod. What else had my parents planned for me?

'And'—Mum's eyes found mine—'if you stop being friends with Paige, we're prepared to look into the idea of you going to St Andrew's next year. I'm not sure how we'll ever afford it, but—'

'"But", Mum?' I yelled. '"But"? Since when is there a "but" when it comes to sticking by a friend? Didn't you always tell me that a good friend stands up for others and stays around to help, even when things get hard?' I stood up and glared at my mother. 'But only the friends who you approve of first, is that it? We'll do that for everyone else, just not my friends because you guys don't like them. That's what you're saying; my friends aren't worth it. And what, you're going to bribe me with what I want most, in order to get what you want out of this?'

'Kathleen Maree!' Dad yelled, standing up.

I stormed out of the room and went straight to the bathroom, locked the door, sat on the toilet and cried. I could hear them back in the kitchen, talking about me. I didn't care. It wasn't fair. They weren't fair. It wasn't fair to me, to Paige, to Keira, even to Megan. Going to St Andrew's had been everything I wanted, but not like this, not if it meant sacrificing my friends to do it. My stomach burned so badly that I turned and vomited the pancakes into the toilet bowl.

***

On Monday Paige was brighter and especially chatty at recess. It was unusually cold for a Queensland winter day, and the line to the tuckshop was long. But since Paige's mum had left, Paige often had money at school and so gathering at the tuckshop had become part of our morning routine—except on the days when her step-dad forgot to give her money. On those days, Keira and I would divvy out our lunches with her or she wouldn't have anything to eat.

Today Paige not only had money, but she had extra, and was going to buy something to say thanks to Keira and I for all the times we'd shared our lunches with her.

'How about a couple of dim sims each?' Paige said as she stepped into the back of the line.

'I can't eat dim sims,' I said. 'They have gluten in them.'

'Urgh,' Paige groaned. 'You and that gluten-free stuff. You probably only say that because you don't like some foods.'

'I do not, Paige.' I hung my head. 'I really love dim sims. I haven't had one in, like, three years.'

Many of the kids in the tuckshop line were rubbing their hands together, jumping up and down to keep warm. Paige disappeared into the sea of faces.

Keira and I stood back waiting for Paige to emerge from within the tuckshop crowd.

'How's detention going?' Keira asked.

'I've been through worse.' I smiled to myself. That sounded like something Adrian would have said.

'What do you do in there?'

'You've had detentions before.'

'But only one-offs. What do you do every day? Is it still those same forms about bullying and stuff? You must have filled in each one a hundred times by now.'

'Yeah, well, I've given up on the forms. The teachers don't bother asking for them anymore.' The line at the tuckshop was starting to shrink. It seemed as though every student that walked past us held a bag of steaming dim sims, warming the noses of those lucky enough to get close enough to smell them. I could almost taste one in anticipation. If Paige came back with one for me, I was going to eat it, regardless of the consequences. I didn't have anything on after school—thanks to the grounding—so I could spend the night on the toilet.

'So, what do you do in detention, then?'

'Well, recently, there's a guy I've been talking to.'

'You met a guy? In detention?'

'Yeah. His name is Adrian.'

'Adrian? Who's Adrian? What year is he in?'

'He's in Year Nine, same as us. In Miss Kelly's form class.'

'Hang on, you don't mean that guy who wears a hoodie all the time? The guy whose dad killed his mum?'

'I thought you said his mum was killed by the Mafia.'

Keira shrugged. 'Whatevs.'

'Well, I don't know anything about that. Besides, he doesn't seem like the type of guy whose dad would kill someone or do drugs and stuff.'

Keira didn't look impressed. 'What do you think a guy whose dad is a murderer would look like?'

'I don't know,' I sighed. I really didn't want to be having this conversation. 'Look, I don't think anyone has killed his mum. He talked about her last week. He was drawing her.'

'That doesn't mean she isn't dead.'

'Keira!'

'Well, it doesn't. So, you're talking to this guy? And you like him?'

'Hardly! He's kinda cool. And cute. And weird.' I shrugged. 'I dunno. Maybe I do like him.'

'Like him how? Like, *like* him?'

I pulled my shoulders up to my ears and held them there for a moment.

'You don't know anything about this guy, Kat.' Keira sounded serious. 'He could be dangerous. Why else would they keep him in detention? They're keeping him away from us for a reason.'

'He's a nice guy. He talks differently than everyone else.'

'Murderers talk different to everyone else too, you know. I've heard nothing but weird stuff about him. You need to be careful. He could tell you anything. He could be a pathological liar for all we know.'

'Who could be a liar?' Paige asked as she joined us, a brown bag of steaming dim sims in her hand.

'That new boy in 9K. Kat's been talking to him in detention.'

'Hoodie boy? That guy's a creep. You should stay away from him, Kat. Who knows what he could drag you into. He's bad news.'

'You guys don't even know him,' I said, turning away. A couple of Grade Seven boys were wrestling on the grassed area. A teacher was trying to separate them.

'Hey,' Paige said, 'I've got some great news, by the way.'

I turned back to see a huge smile spread across Paige's face.

'What is it?' Keira asked.

'As you all know, it's my fifteenth birthday in a couple of weeks. My step-dad said he's going to give me money to go and buy my own presents. So, I was thinking—shopping spree! What do you reckon? We could meet at the shopping centre after school on my birthday and get shakes and doughnuts. My shout.'

'Doughnuts have gluten in them,' I said.

'Oh, we'll get you a hotdog or something, then.' Paige waved her hand around. 'I'm thinking new shoes, new jeans and a couple of new t-shirts are in order. What do you reckon?'

'I won't be allowed to,' I said, my eyes on the ground. 'I'm grounded until the end of the term.'

'But it's my birthday. Surely your parents will make an exception for a birthday?'

'I don't think so, Paige. That's kinda what being grounded is all about.'

'Well, we can wait until the holidays, when you're not grounded anymore. The first Saturday. It will be a double celebration: my birthday and the end of all the punishments for that alcohol-at-school thing.'

'That alcohol-at-school thing, Paige? That *thing* that was your idea, that you actually did, that I have taken the blame for?'

Paige shot me a nasty look. 'Kat,' she said through gritted teeth. 'Ears are listening.'

I looked around, but no one was taking any notice of us. I rolled my eyes. 'Besides,' I said, 'my parents don't want me to have anything to do with you anymore. They probably won't let me, even after being grounded.' I looked at Paige, my eyes growing wide as my hand flew over my open mouth.

'Kat!' Keira put her arm around Paige.

Paige was looking down at the ground. Maybe she hadn't heard what I said?

'Sorry, Paige,' I said, putting my hand out to try to touch her upper arm. 'I...um...I don't agree with them of course, I—'

Paige moved her body backwards so I couldn't reach her. She folded her arms and looked at me with fire in her eyes. The damage had been done; the whites of her eyes turned pink. The bag of steaming dim sims was resting in her hand, tucked up hard against her chest. I waited for the dragon to expel her fire.

'Your parents don't want me hanging around you?' Paige was almost snarling. 'What, they think I'm corrupting their innocent little Mary?'

I looked at Keira who just shrugged.

'I—I guess so.'

'They're trying to protect their darling, lying, back-stabbing daughter, who wouldn't know what a true friend was if she had one screaming in her face?' Spit sprayed from Paige's mouth. Everyone in the tuckshop line turned and looked at us. No one was talking; they were just looking at us, as though we'd stepped off an alien spaceship.

Paige swore then said really loudly, 'I'm going to have a ciggy.'

I looked at Keira, completely dumbfounded, as Paige stormed off towards the school building. I had little idea of what just happened. I wiped my face with my sleeve.

'What's a ciggy?' I asked Keira, who was still standing beside me, frozen.

'It's a cigarette, Kat. Don't you know anything?' Kiera took a packet of gum out of her pocket and removed a piece. 'She's been smoking, like, half a packet a day since her mum left. I spend half my lunchtimes trying to make sure she doesn't get caught.'

My jaw dropped open. 'Where's she getting them from?'

'Her step-dad. After he's passed out every night, she raids his supply.'

'She's gonna hate me,' I said, shaking my head.

'I wouldn't be surprised. What'd you go and say such a mean thing to her for? I thought things were finally starting to get a bit better with her lately. She'd been acting happier and stuff, especially today. And then you had to go and say that to her.'

'I wasn't thinking. It just came out.'

'Yeah, well. Good one. I'd better go and make sure no teachers catch her getting her cigarettes from her school bag. The bell's going to go in a few minutes. The hallway will be swarming with teachers.'

I watched Keira walk off in the direction that Paige had gone. And all I could think was that I never did get a dim sim.

CHAPTER 9

After that little episode, Paige did hate me. She began avoiding me like I was a crank in *The Scorch Trials*—contaminated by the Flare and completely out of my mind. Keira was supporting Paige, and although she told me she felt torn between the two of us, clearly her loyalty was with Paige. It was official: I was friendless at Central High.

I emailed Megan and giving a detailed rendition of what happened that recess in front of the tuckshop. Her reply was full of advice on how to make new friends, including a list of all the strategies that had helped her. It was as if she'd forgotten what life at Central High was like already.

I spent the evenings on my bed crying, praying to the void in my roof space that God would find a way to let me go to St Andrew's with Megan. But praying to God was like throwing a ball up onto the ceiling and it bouncing straight back.

There was so little left in my life to feel happy about. I ran my hand over my wrist where fingernail-shaped bruises stepped up my arm. I rubbed them. What was happening to me? I hardly knew who I was anymore.

At school, first lunch was the worst. I was spending most of my free time on my own. Friendless. A loner. One of those kids who sits by themselves in quiet corners of the yard, reading books. I was glad when the fifteen minutes was over and I could go back to class again. The school yard had become my enemy. Even lunchtime detention was better than a friendless recess. There was nothing worse than being alone.

I admitted as much to Adrian in one detention.

'Detention is better since meeting you,' I said in between bites of my chicken leg. 'At least I have someone to talk to. I just wish detentions weren't so boring. Couldn't they have a few board games to play or something?'

'But then they might have kids being naughty just so they could come to detention. Especially on wet weather days.'

'True,' I laughed, though the idea seemed ridiculous. 'Speaking of, I still don't know what you have done to be in detention every day. What did you do that was so bad?'

Adrian shrugged. 'Nothing.'

'Nothing. Yeah right. Why do you have to keep it a secret? Was it that terrible?'

'What do you think?'

'Well, Keira reckons you have to be in here because of something to do with your family. She reckons it wasn't anything you did, but what they're scared you might do.'

'Because of my family? What has my family got to do with it?'

'She reckons your dad is in prison because he took drugs and your mum was killed by some guy in the Mafia.' I put my head down, not wanting to look at Adrian. I liked him. I didn't want him to be dangerous. I liked him being my friend.

At first, Adrian laughed. Then his face fell and his eyes went dark. 'None of that is true.'

'I thought so. Keira's always saying stuff that isn't true.' I looked at him; his eyes were watery. I quickly looked away again. 'So, you know why I'm here. Why can't I know what landed you in long-term detention?'

'You already know,' Adrian said. 'I've already told you.' His voice was strong, angry.

I looked at him blankly. Then I realised what he meant. 'You're choosing to come to detention every day?'

'Do you blame me, with stories like that going around the school yard?'

I shook my head. 'I guess not. But detention? Really?'

He shrugged. 'It's better than my uncle's office.'

'Your uncle?'

'Mr Dean.'

'Our principal is your uncle?'

'Technically, he's my mum's cousin, not my uncle. But he's heaps older than her and so we've always called him "uncle". I'm living with him for a while. That's why I'm at school here—for now.'

'But, I don't see you with him out of school.'

'Why would you?'

Heat was rising up into my face. 'Well, Mr and Mrs Dean go to the same church as my family.' I didn't like talking about going to church with people at school. It usually ended up in teasing. 'Why don't I ever see you there?'

'I stay home. I don't believe in that stuff.'

'Oh.' I couldn't believe he'd rather spend an hour-and-a-half alone than go to church. At least there was always cake to eat afterwards. 'And what, you hang out in Mr Dean's office when you're not in detention?'

'Yes, I do,' he said as he took a bite of his sandwich.

'But, why? Wouldn't it be better to face the kids in the playground and what they're saying, and maybe make some friends, than hide away like this?'

Adrian didn't say anything.

'It isn't very tough of you.'

'You don't know anything about me or my life. Don't tell me what's tough and what is hiding.' Adrian's face was a storm. 'Sometimes just getting up and going to school, remembering to breathe, reminding yourself to eat, looking for one positive thing in every day, is being tough enough. Facing stupid little kids who don't know anything outside their own front doors is not worth my energy. Uncle Steve and Aunty Vicki understand that.'

'I'm sorry,' I said. 'You're right. I don't know what I'm talking about. I shouldn't have said anything.'

Adrian picked up his pencil and sighed. 'It's okay. I shouldn't have got mad like that.' His cheeks slowly returned to their normal colour.

We were quiet for a moment.

'Don't you get bored?' I asked, my words barely making it out of my mouth. 'Spending all that time on your own?'

'I have my drawing.' A spark shot across Adrian's eyes. 'And besides, you don't ever have to be bored, Miss Kathleen Maree Morrow. Not when you have a mind that you can go away and explore places with.'

I laughed. 'You're weird.' He had soft features when he wasn't angry and I enjoyed watching the way his lips were so purposeful in pronouncing every word when he spoke.

'Seriously. Some of the most fun trips I've had were within the confines of my head.'

I laughed again. 'I don't even know what that means.'

'It means you don't have to leave the room…in order to leave the room.'

'Yeah, 'cause that totally makes more sense.'

'Look, here, hold my hand.'

I looked at him, his hand flat out in front of me, and frowned.

'It's okay, I don't have boy germs.'

I could feel my face exploding into seven different shades of embarrassment. I took his hand.

'Now close your eyes.'

I closed them.

'Take notice of everything in your body, the way you can feel everything—your feet, your knees, your heavy shoulders, your closed eyes. Walk through your body, noticing it, and then forget it again. Focus in on your hand in mine and let everything else become non-existent.'

I focused on our hands together, which wasn't difficult to do because really, that was the only part of my body I could feel. I hadn't held a boy's hand before. Other than Dad's, George's, and boys in kindergarten when we were lining up to go to the library. My hand was becoming warm and I hoped it wasn't going to start sweating. It was already thick and heavy in his.

'Now,' Adrian was saying. 'Imagine we are standing, hand-in-hand, in an enormous pile of leaves. They're multi-coloured. Oranges, reds, yellows, a few greens. They're thick, all the way up to your ankles. They fill the room. They break through the walls and spill out over everything. Now imagine the classroom walls have fallen away. We're standing in a sea of autumn-coloured leaves.'

I formed the picture in my mind. The leaves buried our feet. His hand was still in mine as we stood together. 'You know we don't really have autumn leaves up this end of Australia.'

'Oh—well, can you picture it, still?'

'Sure. We took a train to Armidale in June one year. Dad wanted us to see what being freezing cold was really like. It was one of the best holidays we've ever had as a family.'

'Cool. So, picture the leaves around your ankles and look up, in your mind, and see the blue sky. It's so blue, you have to squint.'

I raised my head as though I was looking up into the sky, my eyes still closed.

'The leaves are rustling under your feet and the sun is

shining down on your face. You are free. We are free, Miss Kathleen Maree. Free to go anywhere we like.'

I breathed in deeply and allowed myself to imagine I was standing in an empty space, with only the leaves under my feet and the blue sky above me. It was freeing. I *felt* free. It had been easy to leave the classroom, to imagine myself away from it. 'Okay. Now what?'

'Where would you like to go?'

'I don't know. A park somewhere?'

'Great idea. But not just any park,' Adrian said. 'Look around you. We're in Central Park in New York City. That's a footpath under your feet. Let's see where it leads. Smell the air. Hear the *witchity-witchity* of a bird in the tree over there.'

Weird. Totally weird. He was definitely bizarre. And yet, something was drawing me in, landing my feet firmly on the ground in New York City.

'It's cold,' I said. 'It must be winter. I can see my breath.'

'It's early morning, too—see how some people look like they're walking to work? Not too many tourists here yet.'

I opened one eye and looked at Adrian. His face looked calm, innocent, his face was so peaceful with his eyes shut, as though he were about to fall asleep.

'Have you been here before?' I asked.

'Not with anyone else.'

I closed my eyes again and breathed in deeply, my heart racing. This was fun, in a peculiar way. 'The trees are beautiful.' I pictured a row of autumn trees with branches hanging over the path like I'd seen in Armidale.

Adrian squeezed my hand. 'Here comes someone on roller skates. Look out! Oh, did you smell that? She must have been eating a hot dog, I could smell the mustard.'

I laughed, peeking over at Adrian again, but his eyes were

still closed. 'Who eats a hot dog this early in the morning? And while they're roller skating?'

'They do all sorts of things in the States.'

I imagined us walking down the path in Central Park, hand-in-hand, like an old couple. I imagined we were 70 years old and we'd lived our lifetimes. We were simply enjoying the rest of our lives with the hard years long behind us. I smiled; perhaps I was as crazy as the boy in the hoodie.

'Oh, I know this part of the park,' Adrian whispered. 'Just around this bend is the lake.'

'Really?' For all I knew, Adrian could have been making most of this up—but it was only pretending, so it didn't matter. I figured I might as well just go with it. 'Look! There's a swan in the middle of the lake.' I smiled, my eyes still shut tight. 'It looks so peaceful on the water.'

'Look up there, Miss Kathleen Maree, up into the sky. Even the city buildings towering over the tree tops are beautiful.' He paused, as though he were enjoying the view. 'That wind is cold but I love how it feels on my face as it brushes my cheek. Like it's giving me a welcoming kiss.'

I tried to feel the breeze on my cheeks too, to see if it would give me a kiss.

'Somewhere around here is a statue of William Shakespeare,' Adrian said.

'Really? That's gotta be some old statue.'

'You love reading. Have you ever read Shakespeare?'

'We did *Hamlet* just before you started at Central High. Oh, and last year we did a film review on 10 Things I Hate About You, which is a rip off of *The Taming of The Shrew*. I think that's by Shakespeare, yeah?'

'I think so. I did something similar at my old school.'

'"To be or not to be—"' I tried to quote *Hamlet* in my best

Shakespearean voice. '"That is the question."'

'I choose…not to be,' Adrian said.

'No you don't.'

'Yeah, you're right,' Adrian sighed. 'But I wish I could choose not to be. It would make living so much easier, if I weren't.'

'Heavy.'

There was silence for a moment, as we sat, holding hands, eyes closed, in our detention prison—but at the same time, free, in the middle of New York City.

'It's really beautiful here,' I said, holding in my mind the picture of the orange-leaved trees hanging over the path. 'I could stay here forever. If the buildings weren't peering out from above the trees, you'd never know you were in the middle of an enormous city.'

'Except for the thousands of people here with us. And the horns honking and people yelling.'

'You can hear all of that?'

'Yep. All of it and none of it. Come on, it's time to go back.'

'Back where?'

'To the classroom.'

'Do we have to?' I whispered.

'Yeah, we do. We can't stay here forever. The bell will ring in a minute. Come on, it's time to go.'

CHAPTER 10

I opened my eyes and arrived back in the classroom first. Adrian was sitting beside me, his eyes still closed, his face peaceful. His eyelids fluttered as he drew himself back to the classroom. I think he really had gone to New York and walked through Central Park with me in that moment.

He looked at me as though he was waiting for me to comment. 'That was amazing. Thanks. I've never been anywhere out of Australia. How do you know so much about that place? Have you been there?'

'No. Maybe I will one day. I read a lot about the States.'

'Well, my dad is obsessed with trains, so all our holidays are to places in Australia we can get to by train. So, if you ever want to go on an imaginary trip to somewhere in Australia on a train—I'm your girl.'

'Really? That's a bit weird.'

'Yeah, well, that's my family.'

'Coming to live with Uncle Steve and Aunty Vicki is the first time I've been out of New South Wales. I've never been on a train before, except maybe when I was little, I think we went to Sydney a couple of times.'

'You're not missing a lot, believe me.'

'Next time we're in detention, I'll take you to San Francisco.'

He let go of my hand. I moved my fingers around. They weren't sweaty at all. 'We'll take a cable car ride around the city, eat at the House of Prime Rib—gluten-free friendly dining, of course.'

I laughed. 'And I'll lock you in one of the prison cells on Alcatraz.'

The bell to mark the end of detention rang out.

'Tomorrow?' I smiled.

'Tomorrow.'

I wondered how I was ever going to wait that long.

***

For the most part, the teachers left Adrian and I alone. None of the teachers had asked for the work I was supposed to be doing during the detention class since I started hanging out with Adrian. Even when we sat up the back, holding hands under the table, they still didn't tell us off. I mean, they had to notice us, whispering to each other, with our eyes closed. Even when there were other kids in detention, they didn't acknowledge us. When we were together, it was as though we were invisible. We were in our own little bubble and everyone just left us alone.

At a time when everything in my life felt as though it was falling apart, Adrian was something to look forward to every day. Our trip to San Francisco had been amazing. He'd held my hand like a true gentleman as I climbed up into the rickety old cable car, which then clunked and groaned as we went up and down hills around the city. We ate American ribs—their strong, smoky barbecue sauce doubling as a facial mask for us both, thanks to Adrian's delightful sense of humour. We hadn't made it to Alcatraz for me to lock him in a cell; Adrian said he didn't like confined spaces and wasn't keen. I suggested we could go back there again one day. Adrian just smiled.

One of my favourite trips was to Seattle. I'd heard of this

city in the U.S. because of an old movie Mum loved to watch. It's got Tom Hanks in it and he lives on a boathouse with his son in Seattle, so I was able to picture what we were doing more clearly. We spent time watching a family build a sandcastle on the beach and a dog chasing a stick his owner was throwing. It looked so free as it bounded across the lapping water's edge, tongue flapping to the side of his mouth, his eyes wide and alert as he searched for the stick. The dog's life seemed so simple. If only people could be so free and easily entertained.

Our time in Seattle was perfect, just like in the movies, but one where Adrian and I were the stars.

'Thank you for coming with me, Miss Kathleen Maree,' Adrian said as we came back into the detention room. 'Travelling is so much better with another person.'

'What, you mean daydreaming?'

'Yeah. It's easier to come back from. It's like, it still feels real, but there's that slight distraction that helps me know that I'm actually grounded in Australia, here with you.'

'I noticed, before I knew what you were doing, that you'd vague-out heaps. Once, some boys were throwing spit balls at you and you didn't even flinch.'

Adrian smiled. 'What's escapism if you can't escape everything?'

In the detention following Seattle, we had ice cream on a beach in California. The day after that, Adrian watched me practise cartwheels on the lawn of the White House in Washington D.C.

Another day we stood at the top of Niagara Falls, allowing the water spray to drench us. Detention was a lovely little bubble that made me feel alive. Eat, chat, visit a place in the U.S.A that Adrian insisted I simply 'had' to visit with him—our lunchtime detentions were the highlights of my day.

I emailed Megan and tried to explain these trips I was taking with a new friend I'd made in detention, but she thought it sounded weird. The more I tried to explain it, the more she suggested I make friends with some of the girls in our class instead. She'd definitely already forgotten what life at Central High was like.

I guess it was inevitable that some of my classmates started to notice things in detention, and on the occasions when Adrian would join me out on the playground. The first time that Adrian decided not to go to Mr Dean's office at recess, he caught me in the corridor, as I was getting something to eat from my bag.

'Miss Kathleen Maree Morrow, I thought I might venture out into the yard this break. Do you have any recommendations on where I should go?'

I laughed. 'You're such an idiot. Come with me, Fred. I'll give you a guided tour.'

We left the building, sharing our snacks as though it was the most normal thing in the world to do. It made me think of Paige, and how I'd always packed extra in my lunchbox for her. Had she so quickly forgotten all the things I'd done for her?

As we stepped out onto the grassed area, it seemed as though the whole school stopped to watch us. Some kids were whispering, others were staring. A few even pointed fingers.

'Wow, Fred. You really know how to wow a crowd.'

'What do you mean? I'm sure they're looking at you.' Adrian smiled as I swatted his arm with the back of my hand. 'Do you think I'm being tough by coming out here this morning?'

'I sure do. Man, I feel like I'm walking beside Justin Bieber or something.'

'Nah, I reckon even Justin would have more fans here than me.'

'What is it with kids and rumours anyway?'

'People will believe what they want to believe, whether there is any truth in it or not.' Sometimes Adrian said stuff that made him sound 50 years old.

'I reckon you have fed the gossip though, by hiding yourself away.' I stole the last of his chips from his lunchbox.

'It only adds to the fun.' Adrian smiled. 'Keeps 'em guessing.'

I walked over to the oval and showed him the place where Keira, Megan and Paige had sat with me while we had that infamous drink. A few Year Seven boys ran past and called out 'Kat's a drunk'. My face grew warm.

Adrian laughed. 'Do they do that often?'

'Oh, not so much anymore. At first, they did. But they forget and move onto the next thing soon enough. Next they'll be chanting that I hang around with murderers.'

'Murderers?'

'Well, you are tarred by association. If your father is a killer, then surely you must be too.'

'Oh, I guess so.' Adrian's voice was sad.

I wished I hadn't said anything.

'But he wasn't you know.'

'What?'

'My dad. The truth is, he was the one who was murdered. But he wasn't into drugs or the Mafia or anything. He was a good man.'

'Geez, Adrian. Sorry.'

'Yeah. Me too.'

We walked in silence for a moment. I pointed out the kids smoking up the back of the oval. You could see them moving their hands back and forth from their faces if you watched for long enough. 'I suppose Paige and Keira have joined in up there.'

'You mean your so-called friends?'

I shook my head. 'They're not my friends anymore. And Megan, my best friend, goes to St Andrew's now. So, I guess you could say I'm friendless at this school.'

'Except me.'

A smile erupted on my face. 'Yeah, I guess so.' We walked in silence for a moment. 'Well, I guess it's just that I don't have any normal friends, then.'

Adrian laughed. 'I'm not that un-normal.'

'Hey, take it as a compliment. Being normal is highly overrated.'

'You should try to make some new friends, though.' Adrian looked serious.

I laughed anyway. 'And why's that?'

'I won't be here for long. I have to go back to my mum soon.'

'Oh? Why?'

'She's in trouble. I need to go back and keep her safe.'

'Why?'

'Because no one else will.'

'Oh.' I wrapped my arms around my stomach and wondered what he could mean. Was it possible there was some truth to the rumour Keira had heard?

***

There were just two weeks until the end of term when I realised how much I was not only enjoying lunchtime detentions, but loathed when they finished. Hanging around with Adrian had become the only part of my school routine I liked.

One day, he'd missed school, and detention was totally deadening without him there. I'd tried going on an out-of-the-classroom trip but it wasn't the same on my own. Adrian had a way of pulling me in and taking me away with him; the way he described things made it feel as though it was all real.

That day, some girls in my class found me sitting on my own at recess.

'Hey, Kat, isn't it?' A girl named Veronica stood over me. She was a nice enough girl, but she was a bit of a Barbie doll.

'Yes, Veronica,' I said. 'You know, we've been in the same form class since Grade Seven.'

She gave a girly little laugh and tossed her blonde hair as she spoke. 'You don't seem to be hanging around those girls anymore. You know, Paige and that other girl.'

'Keira?'

'That's the one. So, what's going on with that?'

The other girls with her all bent in closer, waiting to hear my answer.

'I guess you could say we've gone our separate ways. We don't have much in common at the moment.'

'Seriously?' Another girl, Jessica, spoke up. 'They don't share your love of booze? Or are you not so keen on smokes?'

Veronica gave Jessica a soft slap on the arm. 'Jess, that's hardly friendly.'

'I don't see why that is any of your business,' I said.

'You're totally right, Kat,' Veronica said. 'Just ignore her. She has "outsiders" issues.'

I didn't know what that meant, but I didn't want to know, either. 'Did you want something?'

Veronica smiled. 'We just saw you on your own and thought you might want some new friends. You know, to hang around with?'

'Not really, thanks.' I smiled sweetly. Inside I was completely unimpressed. What did they think? That they would 'save' me, like a charity case, from my current state of non-friend-ness? 'But it was nice of you to offer.' I bit my tongue and looked back at my food, hoping they would go away.

They didn't.

'You know, we saw you out here with your boyfriend the other day,' Veronica said. She sat down beside me, as though she wasn't taking my 'no' to the offer of friendship for an answer.

'He's not my boyfriend,' I said. 'Just a friend.'

'Oh, I see,' she said, and did a little light-clapping-thing with her hands. 'That's great. You see, Mercy here reckons he's really cute. She's into the weird ones.' Veronica smiled and indicated to a very withdrawn-looking girl with black eyeliner plastered onto her face and dyed-black hair. Mercy was in one of the other classes. I'd never spoken to her before, but at least I knew her name. I bet she didn't know mine. 'And well, we wondered whether you thought he'd be, you know, interested in someone like our Mercy.'

'Interested how?' I peered up at Mercy into the sunlight. I couldn't imagine anyone being interested in Mercy, let alone Adrian.

'You know, *interested*,' Veronica repeated. 'She's a lot of fun our Mercy. She thought he might be looking for a date for the graduation dinner.'

I rolled my eyes. 'I doubt Adrian will be going to that. He's not really into that kind of thing.'

'Oh, come on, Kat,' Veronica said. 'Are you sure you're not just trying to keep him all to yourself? You can't say you haven't noticed those gorgeous blue eyes, woven with mystery and intrigue.' She raised her eyebrows as she spoke.

'You know, I can't say I have really,' I said, silently impressed with myself at how easily the lie rolled off my tongue. Not that it was a good thing, that I was suddenly such a good liar. 'And like I said, Adrian's just my friend. But'—I pouted my lips a little—'I don't think he knows of Mercy's existence.' I looked at Mercy, her eyes fixated on the ground beneath her feet. 'Sorry, Mercy, no offence.'

Veronica stood up. 'Well, that's a bit harsh.' She flicked her hair so that it almost hit Mercy in the face.

I looked back to my lunch and ignored the girls' snickers as they walked away. I couldn't wait to have a laugh with Adrian over the whole thing.

CHAPTER 11

The next day, with the promise of a funny story to tell him, Adrian agreed to venture outside again at first break. I was super glad for the company. I took him to the old sports shed that acted as a barrier between the four basketball courts and the footy oval, eager to tell him about my visit from Veronica and 'her Mercy' the day before.

The tin shed was a bit rusty and made funny noises when the wind blew. It backed up to the school fence, but there was enough room to sit behind it without being seen. In the past, the smokers used to sit here, until the teachers caught on and the kids realised they couldn't see when someone was coming. So, they found a new spot to smoke.

I waited until we were sitting on a log before I told Adrian about the conversation I'd had with Veronica the day before. I described the priceless look on poor Mercy's face. Adrian held his stomach he was laughing so hard. I'd never seen him laugh like that before. It was amazing. His whole face lit up and his eyes laughed as much as his mouth did.

'Do you think she might still be interested?' Adrian asked as our laughter eased.

I stopped smiling. 'Why? Don't tell me you're interested?'

His face went serious. 'I don't know. Maybe.'

My face dropped. 'Really? In mousey Mercy?'

'Hey, she could be my potential girlfriend. Don't call her that.'

I looked down to the ground. 'Sorry. I…I didn't think you'd be interested.'

Adrian laughed. 'That was a sweet reaction. Thanks.'

I looked at him and frowned. 'Huh?'

'Your reaction when I said I might be interested in her. That was sweet. You really looked torn by that.'

I frowned at him again. 'What, you were faking an interest to see my reaction?'

He nodded and smiled a big grin that took up half his face.

'That's not very nice.'

He took my hand and stroked it gently. 'Besides, if I'm still here—which I doubt I will be—but if I am, you're the only girl I'd be thinking of taking to graduation.'

I could feel heat rising up my neck. I cupped my free hand around my face to try to hide any blushing.

'Want to go on a trip?'

I gave a half smile and nodded.

Adrian closed his eyes and before long we were in an inflatable raft, flowing down the Colorado River in the Grand Canyon. Walls of red and brown rock towered above us, and tufts of grass lined the banks. The water was so calm you could see the occasional fish swim beneath us.

'Look up there.' Adrian leaned in close and lifted my hand so we were pointing to something in the sky. 'There's a waterfall coming out of the rock face.'

'Wow,' I said. 'It's so beautiful. Where's the water coming from?'

'Must be an underwater stream,' Adrian said.

Even though the sun was hidden, it felt as though it was

shining down on our faces.

Adrian moved closer beside me. With his spare hand, he lifted my chin. I squeezed my eyes even tighter. 'Have you ever been kissed by a boy, Miss Kathleen Maree?'

I shook my head. 'No.'

I could feel his breath sweeping across my lips as he leaned in further, placing his nose so it was almost touching mine. And then, Adrian Jacobs' lips connected with mine, lightly at first, then more firmly. My heart was in my mouth with the taste of his lips on mine. I could feel him smiling as he pulled away.

I didn't know what to say. I just sat there, not daring to open my eyes, in stupid silence like I was a fish flopping out of the water.

I wanted the bell to ring, or for a teacher to come around the corner. But none of those things happened. I didn't know if I was supposed to kiss him back, since he kissed me. And if I wanted him to kiss me again, did I need to make a move?

The thing was, the kiss was nice, but I wasn't too sure what it meant. I'd always thought the boy asked the girl out before there was any kissing. I wasn't sure exactly where that left me. Did I have a boyfriend now?

Adrian was playing with my fingers. We paddled down the river a bit further, neither of us saying anything until Adrian called out a warning shout. 'Look out! The raft is picking up speed and I can see white water ahead.'

'White water? What's that?'

But I didn't need him to explain. Rocks started to appear, sticking out of the water. We began rushing past, picking up more and more speed. I could feel my muscles tightening.

'Adrian!' I yelled, sucking in breath, water splashing up around my face. The raft was bouncing up and down, throwing us. Water was starting to build up at my feet. My face was saturated and my hair was sticking to my face. 'Adrian!' I yelled again.

Walls of coloured rock lunged at us. Rocks underneath tore at the plastic, trying to rip through, trying to swallow us. The paddle I was holding was ripped from my hand and I grabbed onto the raft, trying to keep myself from being overturned by the thrashing water.

I opened my eyes but my eyelashes were soaking wet. Adrian was sitting beside me, but he was still on the Colorado River. I let go of his hand and shook his shoulders. It was raining; we were both getting saturated. 'Adrian!' I yelled again. He finally opened his eyes. 'What did you do that for?' I yelled. I jumped up and started running back towards the classroom. I could feel his footsteps behind me, hear his breath as he followed me. He caught up and grabbed my arm.

I glared at him. 'What did you do that for? We were having a good time when the river was gentle.'

Adrian shrugged. 'That's life, Miss Kathleen Maree. It's not all peaceful trips down quiet rivers. Reality has to hit sometimes.' Water dripped from the edge of his hoodie, catching his eyelashes.

I shook my head. 'No, it doesn't. You did that on purpose. Were you trying to scare me? Well, you did a good job.'

I walked back to my locker where most of the class had gathered. When Mrs Anderson saw me, she yelled at me for being too slow in the rain and accused me of leaving little puddles of water on the floor. I was sent to the nurse's office to dry off, and as I did, I caught a glimpse of Adrian sitting on the floor in his uncle's office.

We'd gone from having the most amazing time together to—what? Had he tried to scare me on purpose? If he had, I couldn't understand why he would do such a mean thing after kissing me.

I didn't see Adrian again until after lunch was over. He walked in with his hoodie dry and pulled up over his head like it always was. I sat in my usual seat beside him, but turned my back to him. I pretended to read my book, but I couldn't have even told you the title, let alone what the book was about.

After a while, a screwed-up piece of paper hit me on the arm and landed on the desk in front of me. I turned to Adrian and frowned. He motioned for me to look at the piece of paper. He'd written me a note:

Miss Kathleen Maree Morrow,

I am sorry.

I am really very sorry.

I didn't mean to scare you—or, maybe I did, subconsciously, because I was scared that you hadn't wanted me to kiss you, or that I shouldn't have kissed you, or that kissing you might have changed things between us. Will you forgive me, please? In exchange for your forgiveness, I will tell you something about myself that almost no one else in my life knows.

From Adrian, trying to be Fred.

I looked at him and nodded. He indicated to me to throw back the piece of paper.

Underneath his first note, he wrote:

As far as I know, my dad had never even tried drugs. He died three weeks before my fourth birthday. I have only a few memories of him. He used to chase me around the house until I was laughing so hard I would fall over, then he'd tickle me. I remember being happy. I remember my mum smiling a lot. And I remember them dancing in our kitchen after dinner.

I wish he hadn't died.

I looked at him as tears burned my eyes. I pulled a pen out of my bag and wrote a reply:

Thanks for telling me that. I will tell you something, too. It isn't something new, but it is something I think about all the time. I hate this school and desperately want to leave. I'm terrified about the thought of still being here next year. But you make things easier. You give me a reason to get up and go to school each day. Sorry, hope that's not too heavy. But it is the truth.

Adrian didn't look at me, he just penned a reply:

That's not too heavy. You know that I like you. But what everyone is saying about me is true: I am dangerous. I don't want you to need me—I can't stay in Fairview. I have to go back to protect my mum. Don't get too close to me, Miss Kathleen Maree. I can't stay here for much longer. I need you to know that, in case I forget.

I frowned and shrugged at him, his words once again a twisted knife in my heart. He went back to concentrating on his drawing.

***

At the dinner table that night, I didn't have much appetite for chicken curry. I didn't have a lot of appetite for anything, other than thoughts of Adrian Jacobs. My mind was preoccupied with him; my heart, too busy dealing with strange new feelings. I couldn't possibly fit another thing in.

George was singing a song at the top of his voice. It was a tune I'd heard before, but he was singing completely different words and I couldn't work out either song. The occasional mention of Batman made me wonder if he was just making something up. I was glad for the white noise, leaving me alone with my thoughts. Everyone else at the table, though, was looking at him, frowning.

'What?' he asked, grinning, like as if he knew exactly what he was doing.

I picked again at my food.

'You not hungry tonight, sweetheart?' Mum asked.

I shrugged.

'Oh,' Rebecca said. 'She probably won't eat for a month. Haven't you heard? Kat has a boyfriend.'

CHAPTER 12

'What?' Mum, Dad and I all said at the same time.

My heart leapt into my mouth. There was no way Rebecca could possibly know Adrian had kissed me at school earlier that day! 'What are you talking about?' I asked.

'You and that boy who wears the hoodie all the time,' Rebecca said. 'Word is, he's your boyfriend.'

'Booger!' George said from beside me, displaying a large, green, solid mass that had been extracted from his nose by his right middle finger. He thrust it into the centre of the kitchen table, so it was hanging perilously close to our plates of food. Still, everyone ignored him. All eyes were on me.

'Who said?' I could feel a knot in my stomach. Was the awesome bubble that I'd been living in about to burst?

'That Paige girl you used to be friends with was telling everyone at the bus shelter. She said something about him being your new "habit", since the drinking thing hadn't worked out for you.'

'What?' I shot to my feet.

'Rebecca!' Mum said, almost at the same time. 'I hope that you told her to stop spreading such tommyrot.'

'Well...' Rebecca went quiet.

'Who is this boy in a hoodie anyway?' Dad asked.

I sat back in my chair as my head began filling with a

cloudy, thick gas. 'He's a new boy in my year level, in one of the other classes, but we're in the same math class,' I said, sitting back down. My head was spinning. 'He wears a hoodie all the time, even when it's hot, so all the kids just call him that. But his name is Adrian.' I looked at Mum and then Dad. 'He's living with Principal Dean at the moment.'

Mum looked at Dad, who nodded slowly. I could see she wasn't terribly happy with this revelation.

'And, he's not your boyfriend, though. Right?' Dad asked.

'Not really,' I lied. I felt bad as I watched Mum's face relax. But, I wasn't sure what exactly to tell them. I didn't even know. Adrian had kissed me, so did that mean he was my boyfriend? I wished they'd asked me the question yesterday—then it would have been easy to answer.

'Kathleen,' Dad said. He had that whole '*tell us the truth or we might be tempted to kill you*' sound to his voice. 'Is Adrian your boyfriend?'

'Well, he is in my math class and we've been hanging out together at recess sometimes. We started talking because he's usually in detention with me at lunchtime.'

'Great place to get yourself a boyfriend,' Rebecca said under her breath.

'What about your friends?' Dad asked.

'What friends, Dad? Paige and Keira don't like me anymore. You said I wasn't allowed to be friends with them, remember? I told Paige you guys don't like her and she got totally mad and hasn't spoken to me since.'

Mum put her head down in her hands and shook her head. 'Kat,' she mumbled.

'What?' I asked.

'That's not the sort of thing you go around telling people,' Dad said.

I shrugged. 'I didn't mean to. It just slipped out.' I played with my curry on my plate. 'They don't talk to me. Keira did a bit at first, but Paige doesn't at all. So, Adrian is really weird and stuff, but he's nice and doesn't have any friends either. We kinda just ended up hanging out together.'

'But he's not your boyfriend,' Mum said.

'Why? What's the big deal if he is or not?'

'Booger!' George yelled, his face red and swollen, his body and finger still extended over the table. Mum reached behind, grabbed a tissue and in one swoop, removed the booger from George's finger. George smiled and sat back down in his chair, placing his Batman doll in his lap, pretending to feed it some of his curry.

'Because,' Mum said calmly, as though she wasn't holding a booger in the scrunched-up tissue in her hand, 'if he was, we would want to know about something like that.'

I picked up some chicken and chewed it slowly in my mouth. I must have got a piece of chilli. My mouth started to burn.

'So, Kat,' Dad said over the noise of my coughing. 'What you're telling us, is there is a new boy in Year Nine, who is living with Mr Dean, and he's your new friend at school. Just friends, but a boy that is a friend. Is that right?'

I nodded, my eyes watering. I guess what Dad said was true enough. There was no way I was going to tell my parents a boy had kissed me. Besides, it was nothing serious. Right?

'Then why are your eyes watering?' Mum looked at me suspiciously. 'You'd better not be lying to us again.'

'It's just the curry is hot,' I said, waving my hand in front of my mouth. I gulped down a mouthful of water. 'I'm not lying. I don't have a boyfriend.' Well, as far as I knew, Adrian was not my boyfriend. And the curry *was* hot.

'Seriously, Kathleen,' Mum said, while still finishing a mouthful. 'If we find out you've been lying to us about this boy, too—'

I glared at Mum. She stopped talking.

'Kaff-lee,' George said. 'Watch me.' He put his face down so it was even with the table, pulled his plate in close and began shoveling curry into his mouth. His plate was empty within moments, and he sat and chewed his food with a big grin on his face.

'Your turn,' he said, with a mouth still full of curry. Some rice flew out onto the table. I giggled, which made him smile more, and another lot of curry fell from his mouth. Some even landed in Rebecca's dinner. She started screaming.

'George!' everyone else yelled in unison. *Way to take the heat off me, George.* What a legend my little brother could be.

***

On Monday morning, I got to school right on the bell. Adrian wasn't lining up for math class or in his usual seat up the back. I was about to ask Mrs Kelly if she knew where he was, when he walked into class, five minutes late. He didn't look at me.

All morning, while we were working on a revision sheet for an upcoming math test, he sat in his usual spot and ignored me. I was angry at him—ignoring me was worse than yelling at me, especially since I had no idea what I had done to upset him. I pretended to drop my pencil and bent down to pick it up, banging his leg with my arm. Still nothing; it was as if we'd never spoken. As if I were invisible and so was he, but now for some reason, he couldn't see me anymore.

I pulled a piece of paper out from my folder and wrote across the top of it: *What's going on with you?* I slid it across his table so it partially covered the drawing he was doing. He screwed it up and put it into his desk drawer. I frowned and coughed to try to get his attention. But he ignored me. He was my only friend—my only friend! I didn't know whether to be hurt or sad or really angry.

At break, I hung back and waited for Adrian to leave the classroom, but he brushed by me, heading straight towards Mr Dean's office.

'Hey!' I called after him. He didn't respond. How could he kiss me one day, then act as though I didn't exist? I needed to breathe deeper, to catch my breath somehow. I thought he cared about me!

I ran after him and grabbed him by the arm. 'Hey, what are doing?' I yelled. 'Why are you ignoring me?'

He looked out from under his hoodie, his eyes red and dark around the edges.

I stood back, shocked. 'What happened to you?'

He shook his head. 'Leave me alone.'

'Adrian! Please, you can at least tell me what I did wrong.'

Adrian lifted his head and looked me in the eyes. 'It's not about you, Kat.'

Kat? Since when was I only Kat to him? 'I'm not going to leave you alone until you tell me what's going on,' I said.

He stood still, his shoulders slumped forwards.

'Please, Fred?' I dared to smile a little.

His eyes sparkled for the briefest of moments. He sighed. 'I don't want to get you involved in my life. I'm not going to be around for much longer and you're just going to get hurt. It's better if we leave each other alone.'

'What do you mean?'

'I mean, I'm going back to live with my mum. I can't stay here forever. I have to go and look after her, like I told you. Soon.'

'Why does she need looking after?'

'Because she is in danger,' Adrian said.

I gasped. 'Not the Mafia?'

'No, Miss Kathleen Maree, not the Mafia.' Adrian gave me a little smile. 'Look, I'll tell you, but not here, okay? Meet me on the steps outside the art room.'

I headed straight there. They were in a section of the school hardly anyone went, unless they actually were an art student. Some girls were sitting around on the other side of the asphalted area, but they wouldn't bother us. They'd hardly even notice anyone sitting here; it was kind of dark with the veranda overshadowing the steps.

Before long, Adrian appeared beside me. His hoodie was pulled right up over his head so his eyes were barely visible.

'What's going on?' I asked. 'Is your mum okay?'

'She is for now. But not for long.'

'Why? What's happening?'

Adrian sighed. 'After my dad died, Mum was pretty messed up. She got a boyfriend who was bad news. He wasn't nice to her, or to me and my brother. That's why Tom left.'

'Is Tom your brother?'

Adrian nodded. 'And that's why Uncle Steve came and got me and brought me here.'

'What, because he thought you were in danger?'

'Yes. No. Sort of.' Adrian shook his head. 'Mum's boyfriend is in jail. Uncle Steve came and got me because Mum was in such a bad way and Uncle Steve reckoned she wasn't looking after me. He found out about what had been happening because of the court case, and he'd been visiting us and stuff. But once Tom left, things got worse. Between Uncle Steve and Mum's social worker, they decided I needed to go live with Uncle Steve for a while, or risk me ending up in foster care.'

'Do you think she wasn't looking after you?' I asked.

'Pretty much,' Adrian said, dropping his eyes to the floor. 'She's got some issues.' He let out a heavy sigh. 'Instead of buying food and stuff, Mum'd blow half her money at the bottle shop.'

'Really? That's terrible. It sounds like it was just as well you left to live with Mr and Mrs Dean.'

Adrian's face contorted. 'She's still my mum and I love her, alright?' He stood up and walked around for a few seconds, his hands fidgeting at his sides. He came and sat back down. 'She's getting herself cleaned up now, she's promised me. She's moved town to get away from the bad influences and is applying for jobs. She's trying to get herself a place with a couple of bedrooms. Uncle Steve and Aunty Vicki said they'll let me go back to her soon. He told me so yesterday after we went to see our case manager.'

'But, so, why is she in danger?'

Adrian shook his head. 'No one knows just how much danger she is in, except me—and Tom, but Tom doesn't care. Not even Mum gets it; that's why she needs me to protect her. You see, there's no point in us being friends. I'm not staying. I have to go back to her.'

'Well, I don't see why you have to go back to her. It doesn't sound like she's been a very good mum so far. And especially if she is in some sort of danger.'

'Yeah, well, that's just the way it is.'

'Well, I think you're being mean saying we can't be friends anymore. That's just dumb.'

Adrian stood up, put his head down and headed in the direction of Mr Dean's office, his hands jammed tightly into the pockets of his hoodie. I sat on the step and cried.

At lunchtime, I sat across from Adrian in the detention room and watched him close his eyes and go off to another place—somewhere other than the detention room—on his own. I pretended to be studying for the history test we were having after lunch.

***

By the end of the school day, I was a mess. I couldn't remember anything about the Aztecs or their influence on our society. I had ignored Mr Wally by accident three times because I was having trouble focusing on what he was saying.

I couldn't stand the thought of Adrian being at school and not being my friend.

So that afternoon, rather than going to meet my mum straight after school like I was supposed to, I followed Adrian into Mr Dean's office.

CHAPTER 13

I shut the door to the principal's office behind us. Adrian turned and looked at me with a mixture of shock and anger on his face. I wasn't sure if he was upset because I had followed him in there, or because I was invading his space. I didn't care. There was no way I was going to let him get away with treating me like he had. He was my friend. My only friend in this horrible place and I wasn't going to let him just walk away without telling me why first.

'Look,' I said, squeezing my cheeks with the palms of my hands as I tried to form the right words in my head. 'I am sorry about your dad dying. I couldn't imagine anything worse to go through than something like that. My dad had a heart attack a few years ago. He could have died if the doctors hadn't got him into surgery straight away. It scared the living daylights out of me. Look at me'—I held out my hand—'I still shake every time I talk about it.'

'I didn't know that.' Adrian's shoulders slumped. 'But that's—'

'I'm sorry, too, that your mum met her boyfriend and that she's so messed up, and that he hurt you both. And I'm sorry I said that it's probably a good thing that you're not living with her anymore. That wasn't very nice of me to say.'

Adrian nodded. 'True. But—'

'But,' I said holding my hand up to make him listen to me.

'The thought of you being here in this school and not being my friend is scarier than anything else in my life I have faced. I already lost Megan, and you are the only good thing left. So, I am sorry that you don't think we should be friends anymore because we might end up getting hurt, but that is not what I think.'

My hands ended up on my hips and I was talking really loudly. Adrian was looking at me with his mouth slightly open.

'I think we should still be friends'—my voice was shaking—'because we like each other and because we get to do cool things together, like go on big daydreaming trips and share our lunches, and because you remember that I'm gluten-free and because you care about me more than any of my other friends have ever really cared for me before. And if we can't be friends at school, if you are going to ignore me, then I have no reason to come to school anymore and that sucks, maybe even more than it sucked when Megan went to St Andrew's.'

It was then that Adrian laughed. I didn't know whether to be mad, or to laugh as well.

He came over and stood really close to me. 'You like me?' Adrian said. He wrapped his arms around my waist, pulling me in close until we were in an embrace.

I closed my eyes and rested my head on his shoulder. I noticed we were almost exactly the same height. 'You could do with a growth spurt, you know, Fred,' I said.

He was chuckling in my hair. I stepped back and put my hand out for him to shake. 'Friends? It doesn't need to be anything more than just that. We can be friends. Even friends who live in different states, if you do move back to live with your mum.'

He took my hand. 'I dare not say no.'

***

'What's the worst thing you've ever done?' Adrian asked so

simply, so calmly, like he was asking more about the weather than my moral standing.

It was Friday, so no detention, and Adrian was braving the whole day with me out in the yard. We'd had a bet that if he couldn't get Mrs Anderson to crack a smile during our Wednesday afternoon revision test—and believe me, Mrs Anderson took her revision tests incredibly seriously—he'd have to spend the whole day in the yard with me on Friday. As we'd sat at the class set of laptops ready to do the online quiz, I noticed Adrian had signed in as Fred. He hadn't been successful in making Mrs Anderson smile, but he had me in stitches.

I pondered Adrian's question. 'Worse thing I've done, or worse thing I've been caught doing?'

'Hmm, I think, worse thing you've been caught doing,' Adrian said. 'And if it isn't very interesting, then we can do when you weren't caught.' He winked at me.

The old concrete tunnel we sat in was terribly uncomfortable. We weren't supposed to come to this section of the school without a teacher, let alone be sitting in the old piece of concrete tunneling. Therefore, it made a great place to sit if one wanted a little privacy. It wasn't the first time I'd ignored the red plastic barrier walls around it and sneaked inside during a recess or lunchtime.

'Well, then, I guess that's easy,' I said, taking a bite of marinated chicken leg. 'The worse thing I've ever been caught doing is the thing that landed me in detention.'

'Do you regret it now?' Adrian asked.

'Yes,' I said. 'I've never regretted something more in my life.' I was silent for a moment. 'Except, maybe not as much as I did at first. I wouldn't have become friends with you if I hadn't got half a term's worth of lunchtime detentions.' I smiled, then took another bite of my chicken.

'I guess you'd still be friends with that Paige girl, though, if that was the case.'

I shrugged. 'I guess so.' I sighed. 'Or not. When I think about it, I'm not sure how long my friendship with Paige would have lasted, once Megan had left the school.'

'Why's that?' Adrian was eating a sandwich, but not the way a normal person eats one. He was plucking small pieces off the edges, then shoving them into his mouth as though his teeth wouldn't open wide enough.

'Oh, I don't know. I guess I see now that she wasn't a very good friend to me. She got me into trouble sometimes and used to tease me and stuff.'

'Like how?'

'Just calling me names and that. She had this one name for me. Mary. Whenever she thought I was not being adventurous or being too cautious, she'd call me Mary.'

'Mary?'

'Yeah, you know, Jesus' mother, who is like the saint of all saints. I reckon Paige thought that because my family goes to church, and me not wanting to do the wrong thing and get into trouble...I dunno.'

'I thought that Mary's a Catholic Church thing,' Adrian said.

I raised my eyebrows at him. 'I thought you weren't into all that church stuff.'

'I'm not,' he said, looking down at his sandwich. 'But that doesn't mean I don't know anything. My dad was Catholic. I think my grandparents took him when he was a kid.'

We ate in silence for a few moments.

'You know, apparently, Paige has been spreading rumours about me,' I said.

'Oh? Like what?'

'Well, that I was addicted to alcohol, for one thing.'

Adrian scoffed. 'As if anyone is going to believe a high school kid's an alcoholic—let alone you.'

'And,' I said. 'That you and I are dating.'

I looked at Adrian out of the corner of my eye. A smile crept onto his face. 'Well, she's a bit right, 'ey?'

I giggled. 'Rebecca was telling me about these rumours at the dinner table the other night and Mum and Dad were, like, totally shocked. They were all like, "Well, is he your boyfriend?" and all that kind of stuff. Fortunately, George spat his dinner halfway across the table and diverted the attention off me.'

Adrian laughed. 'What did you ever see in that girl that you were her friend all those years?'

I shrugged. 'I guess she wasn't so bad when we first became friends. She just kinda got more and more mean as time went on.'

'Like crabs in a cooking pot,' Adrian said.

I laughed. 'Like what?'

'You know, crabs. People put them into the pot while the water is cold and put it on a slow heat. The crab doesn't notice the water is getting hotter and hotter until it dies.'

'That's so mean! How could someone do something like that? Poor crabs.'

Adrian laughed. 'I don't know if they do it anymore. I think it's just a saying now.'

'Oh, good,' I said. I ran my hands down my school uniform. 'Paige hurt me. We'd been friends for a long time, and there were times when we'd have little fights and stuff. But I never thought she'd dump me as quick as she did. Especially after all I did for her.'

'Why?' Adrian asked. 'What did you do for her?'

I just sat with my head down, not saying anything.

'Was it Paige who brought the alcohol to school that day? Were you covering for her?'

I didn't say anything.

'Uncle Steve was right, wasn't he? You didn't bring that alcohol to school and that rotten excuse for a friend of yours did. You should say something. Paige is a big girl. She needs to take the rubbish that comes from treating other people like rubbish.'

'You don't know that's what happened. You weren't there. And how do you know that's what Mr Dean thought happened?'

Adrian's cheeks turned pink. 'I was in the office when Mr Wally came in. I was sitting in the room when Mrs Anderson and Uncle Steve talked about how they reckoned it was Paige, not you. I heard him saying if you didn't own up to the truth, that he would make you do detention for the rest of the term. Why do you think I started attending lunchtime detentions all of a sudden?'

'You started going to detention because of me?'

'Well, I couldn't think of any other way to get your attention.'

'I don't understand why you'd do that.'

'I'd never met a girl like you before. You were so kind and thoughtful, and so beautiful. You seemed to me to be the perfect girl. I thought I'd like to know you a bit.'

I shook my head. 'Is that why you stuck your finger up at Paige when you walked out of Mr Dean's office?'

Adrian smirked. 'I can't say I've ever liked that girl.'

'That's not really fair. I mean, everyone has their issues and especially Paige, you know. She's got heaps going on in her life. You don't know her.'

'There you go—perfect example.' Adrian took my hand and ran his finger over my palm. 'Here's this girl, spreading rumours around the school about you and ignoring you, and you're defending her. And, can I just add, that's just the rumours you know about—it's possible there is even more she is making up behind your back.'

I shook my head. 'Yeah, well, maybe. But just because she's not being nice to me doesn't mean I get to say not nice things about her.'

Adrian smiled. 'Kathleen Maree, you have such a good heart. Don't ever let the world steal it away from you.'

I laughed. 'Seriously, Fred, sometimes you sound like you're a hundred.'

'I do have a year, plus a couple of months, on you.'

'Well then,' I said, smiling. 'I guess age can make all the difference.'

Adrian's face fell serious. 'If you've been lying, it can be good to get the truth out, because small lies usually end up needing a bodyguard of bigger lies to protect them.'

I frowned. 'What? Why would you say that?'

'I've learnt things from my own experiences, I guess. And, well, the most logical thing is you're covering for Paige. You're too good a kid to do something as stupid as bring alcohol to school, especially if there was any chance of getting your friends in trouble. Paige, however...'

What the...? Too good a kid? A thousand thoughts raced through my head. Mr Dean...Adrian joining me in detention... Being sat up the back next to Adrian in math...The detention teachers leaving us alone to do what we wanted.

Sickness flooded over me, stealing the blood from my face and making my teeth ache. 'A kid? You called me a kid?' I practically spat on him as I raised my voice. 'Did Mr Dean put you up to this? Did he ask you to befriend me, to find out the truth about what happened with the alcohol that day at school?'

Adrian looked genuinely surprised. 'What? No.'

'Really? Because it's looking really suspicious right now. Why else would the teachers on detention duty leave us alone up the back of the classroom, not ever asking us for the work we're supposed to do in there? What, is Uncle Steve putting the pressure on you to find out the truth now the end of the term is so close?'

Adrian sat back from me and looked me in the eyes. 'Uncle

Steve didn't set me up for anything.'

I stared at Adrian, trying to see any hint of truth. Was it possible our whole friendship had been based on him trying to get to the point where I would confess what really happened that day to him? I couldn't believe it. It wasn't possible; he was my only friend. My only friend at this stupid, rotten school!

'I need to think,' I said, starting to make my way out of the tunnel. 'I need to know you aren't being my friend because the teachers have asked you to.'

Adrian took a deep breath. 'Look, wait, Kathleen. You're right. There is some stuff you should know about me, stuff that I probably should have told you earlier.' I sat back down, halfway between Adrian and the tunnel entrance, and indicated for him to continue. 'The teachers leave me alone, but it isn't anything to do with you. It's because Uncle Steve asked them to. So long as I'm not disturbing anyone else, they're supposed to let me do what I want at school. I haven't been disturbing you, have I?'

'Sort of. Maybe.' Disturbing wasn't the right word to use. Saving my sanity, maybe.

'Look, please. I've always liked you, Miss Kathleen Maree Morrow. From the moment I saw you I thought you were the most beautiful girl I'd ever seen. I watched your friends do mean things and, I don't know, but you were never mean back. You just waited until they got over themselves and then you'd forgive them and move on. You were the kind of person I thought I would like to talk to, because I'd never known someone who was faithful like that. I didn't mean to make you my friend, I didn't even want to. I have never wanted to see you get hurt. Don't you get that?'

I smiled a little, my heart soaring with the understanding that Adrian, the amazing and patient and strange and weird boy beside me, saw things in me I'd never been able to see in myself. And nice things! Things that he thought were admirable, things that made me a worthwhile person. I inched my way back towards him. He reached out and took my hand, just like we did when we went exploring places together. And I remembered how much I had come to trust the boy who wore a hoodie.

'I'm sure that is why the teachers have left us alone, because they could see that we were good for each other. Maybe Uncle Steve saw that too, I don't know. I wasn't spying on you, not ever, not for Uncle Steve anyway.' He paused and gave a little smirk. 'There may have been a few times I watched you from a distance, but that was for me—no one else. Like, I'd watch how you're allergic to grass, but you'd still sit out on the oval with your friends and not say anything. And that day when you got into trouble with Mr Wally, I wanted to rescue you. I wanted to tell Uncle Steve to leave you alone, that you wouldn't do something like that. I didn't want to see you get hurt, or to be sad.' He wiped his hand across his face, ruffling the small fringe beginning to stick out from under his hoodie.

My cheeks were burning, but I didn't care whether he could see it in the dim light or not. 'I like how you're growing your hair.'

His soft blue eyes sparkled from under his hoodie, even in the darkness of the tunnel. 'Mum always liked my hair longer.' He pushed the hoodie back off his face a little more. 'I hoped you might, too.'

I put my hands on my chest and felt my heart thumping. I didn't get it; I was nothing special. My hair was always messy and I had a thousand black heads around my nose. There wasn't anything about the way I looked that would make a boy like me.

And yet, it seemed, one did.

CHAPTER 14

When I got home that night, I took out my school diary to get Mum to sign it and found a folded note. It had 'Miss Kathleen Maree' written on the front. My heart pounded. What was it about a written note that was so much more personal than an email?

'Kat, can I talk to you please?' Mum asked as I started towards the bathroom—the only room in the house with a lock on the door.

I looked from the note to my mum and back to the note. 'Okay, sure.' Mum was sitting at the kitchen bench, surrounded by trays of chocolate brownies. 'You've been baking?'

Mum didn't bake much. She said that when George was born she was still recovering from the shock of Dad having had a heart attack—and one of the side effects was not having the energy to bake much anymore. 'Thought I'd give it a go.' She cut a small slice off one of the slabs. 'What do you think?' I'd no sooner put it in my mouth when George, complete with a slowly deteriorating Batman doll, appeared around the corner. That kid could smell sugar being eaten from a mile off.

'Oh! Me too!' George shrieked.

As melted chocolate filled my mouth, I cut a half piece and handed it to George. 'It is good, Georgie.'

'Mmmmm.' George pulled a tiny crumb from his mouth

to feed Batman.

'One lot will be for the Harrisons,' Mum said. 'But the other is for us.'

'Why's that? Is Mrs Harrison sick again?'

Mum nodded. 'They're running tests. John is coming back home to look after her.'

'Oh,' I said. Mrs Harrison was old, but not as old as my gran. Everyone seemed to know her, and she remembered the names of everyone at church. She had a way of making me feel special just in the way she always said hello. Like she cared. 'That's so sad.'

'Sure is.' Mum pulled out a notepad from under her cookbook. She licked her fingers and turned some of the pages, a determined look on her face. 'You know, your birthday is fast approaching.'

'Yeah, I know.' Though I'd been doing my best to forget about it.

'Well, have you thought about what you might like to do to celebrate?'

'You mean, like, what to have for dinner that night?' Birthday tradition number one in our house was on your birthday you get to decide the evening meal.

'Yeah, there's that. But since it's during the school holidays, I thought you might like to do more than just a family dinner.'

'Are you talking about a party?'

Mum nodded. 'Would you like one?'

'I didn't think I'd get to do anything like that. You know, after everything that has happened this term.'

'You made a silly choice, Kat, and the consequences were what they were. We're not going to keep punishing you for it. I'm proud of how much you seem to have grown up in the past few weeks.'

That was unexpected. Was it true?

'Thanks, but I think, maybe, I'm not so keen for a party this year. I'm a bit short on friends for a start.'

'Horse feathers,' Mum said. 'You're a lovely girl with plenty of friends if you look hard enough.' She ran her hand over my hair. 'But, we had thought you might feel that way. So, your dad and I figured you could choose two friends and we'll all go to a theme park for the day. You know, that could be fun?'

A broad smile erupted across my face. 'Are you serious? That would be brilliant! But, it sounds expensive.'

Mum smiled. 'We've been putting money away for a while, to do something special for you this year. We feel like you're sometimes the one who misses out in the family, you know, being the middle child and everything.' Heat was rising to my cheeks. I couldn't believe my parents had done something like that for me.

'Thanks, Mum!' I kissed her on the cheek. A million thoughts started racing through my mind. There was so much to do! I'd start by emailing Megan. And Adrian—how would that go down with Mum and Dad? I really wanted to ask him. It wouldn't be fun if I couldn't have both Megan and Adrian there.

Dad walked into the room. 'She liked the theme park idea?'

Mum nodded.

'Who will you ask?' Dad stood beside Mum and placed his arm around her waist.

The word 'Adrian' caught in my throat and made me cough. 'I'll have a think about it.'

'Well,' Dad said. 'Just so you know, if you want to invite the boy staying with Mr Dean, we're okay with that. It might be nice to meet him, actually.'

My heart did a full somersault. I grinned and nodded.

'There's more we want to talk to you about,' Mum said, leafing through to a new page in her notebook. 'We were going to wait until your birthday to tell you…but, we have some good news for you.'

I sat down at the breakfast bench.

'We think,' Dad said, 'that we've found a way for you to go to St Andrew's.'

'Not until next year,' Mum added. 'But we made some phone calls and it turns out St Andrew's has a special fund for pastors' families. We can apply, and if they accept us, we can send you to the school at reduced fees. In fact, it will only cost us a bit more than sending you to Central.'

'What—why? Because Dad works for the church?'

'Yes,' Mum said.

'But, what about my record? Like, won't they say no because of the alcohol-at-school thing?'

'They would put you on a behaviour contract for the first year,' Dad said. 'But otherwise, they didn't seem too phased about it. Apparently, it isn't all that uncommon in pastors' kids.'

I scratched my head. 'So, you're saying I can go to St Andrew's next year?'

'Not definitely. We'll fill out the paperwork and start the application process, but there will be a few conditions,' Mum said. 'It is still going to cost us more, not to mention the extra travelling we'll have to do to get you there, and we'd have to find a way for you to have your own laptop. So, you'll need to agree to a few things first.'

'Like?'

'Behavioural conditions,' Mum said. 'No more bad decisions.'

'Can you be more specific?'

'Well, no more lying. Or making stories up.'

'Done!' I was finished with all that anyway.

'And then there's hanging around with people who are going

to have a good, positive influence on you.'

'At Central? Come on, do such people exist?' I shook my head.

'This is about more than just friends, Kat. We want to see you making good choices. If you can show us you can do that, you can go to St Andrew's. That's your carrot.'

'My carrot?'

'Yeah, you know, something to look forward to, like a horse with a carrot dangling in front of it. Make the right decisions, make the kind of choices we would approve of, and we'll send you to St Andrew's next year.'

It sure was a big carrot. A big, orange, shiny carrot that had all the goodness of what I'd been wanting since Megan left. I couldn't wait to email her and tell her about it. Except, if I went to St Andrew's, and Adrian stayed with Mr Dean, I'd be leaving him at Central on his own. I couldn't do that to him. But he'd never said anything about staying—in fact, he'd only talked about the opposite. Then I remembered the note.

I felt the smoothness of the paper in my pocket. I held it carefully between my fingers as I hurried to the bathroom. I locked the door, put the lid down on the toilet and pulled the note out.

I don't know if it means anything to you, but I want you to know that I believe you did not bring alcohol to school. So, I am going to continue to believe my version of the truth, which is that you didn't do it. I want you to know that. That way, if you or I die tonight, we both know that you know that I know the truth, which is this: You didn't do it.

And even if you did that which I know you didn't, it doesn't change my high opinion of you. Not even a little bit.

I giggled and folded the note back up. I didn't always understand everything that Adrian said, but I loved the way he made words and sentences sound mysterious. He made me want to know more and understand more. He made me want to travel the world to see the amazing places we'd 'been to' together in our detention room prison. He made me want to understand all those big words and complicated sentences. He made me want to be someone else—the someone that he already believed me to be.

CHAPTER 15

'You know, it's almost the end of term,' I said the next day, grabbing Adrian's pencil and starting a doodle on the back of the detention sheet. 'There's only two detentions left after today.'

At the front of the room, Mrs Kelly shuffled her newspaper before clearing her throat. She looked at me and smiled, then went back to reading what looked like the comic section.

'Yeah, and then it will be school holidays. You'd be happy about that, wouldn't you?' I looked around the now-familiar detention room. It no longer held fear over me. It didn't even look as bleak as it had in the beginning. It held warm memories now. Adrian memories.

'I don't know. I won't get to see you as much, not like this anyway, and that makes me sad.' Heat rose to my cheeks as I stole a sideways glance at Adrian. I stifled a nervous giggle. 'It's my birthday in the holidays. I'm looking forward to that.'

'What are you doing for it?'

'Mum said I could ask a couple of friends to come to one of the theme parks on the Gold Coast for the day. I'm thinking Movie World.'

'Really? That's awesome. You're so lucky.' Adrian grabbed his pencil out of my hand and began scribbling pictures of three-pronged cactus bushes and tufts of dry grass. 'I've never been to a theme park before. Movie World has a ride called Wild West Falls.' He drew a plank of wood and wrote 'Wild West Falls' on it, then added a few bullet holes. 'It's set in Dodge City in Kansas, which is mid-western U.S.A. You so should totally go on that ride while you're there.'

'I will. But you know, you could come too. Mum said I could ask two friends. I asked Megan already and I thought, maybe, that you might like to come as well. Mum said it would be okay.'

Adrian looked at me for a moment. Something like fear flickered across his face. 'I dunno, Miss Kathleen Maree. I've never met your parents, or Megan, or Rebecca and George.'

'Well, if there is one thing for sure, you don't need to worry about George. He loves everyone. All you have to do is slip in a couple of sentences about Batman and he'll be your best friend for life.'

'George likes Batman?'

'Obsessed might be a better term,' I said. 'He's driving us all mad with this one doll that my grandma made for him. He sleeps with it and everything.'

'Okay, George is easy. But what about everyone else?'

'Why don't you come to church on Sunday? Then you can meet my family. And it doesn't matter that you haven't had much to do with Megan. She's cool. You remember her from math class, yeah?'

'She's pretty smart.'

'That's Megan.' *Megan, who only lives 25 minutes away but I haven't seen since, well, since she left Central.* 'You'll get along with her no worries.'

'I'll think about it. But thanks for asking.'

'If you don't, we might not see each other until next term.'

Adrian nodded. 'Chances are I won't be here next term, too, if I can get hold of Mum.' He looked at me as I held my breath, tears stinging my eyes. 'Oh, but you know, Movie World sounds like heaps of fun.' He quickly looked away.

Stupid boys that never understand girls and how they're feeling. Stupid boys that never know what to say, or how to say it. Except usually Adrian did. 'It wouldn't be the same without you,' I said. 'I really want you to come.'

He smiled, before turning his piece of paper over to start a new drawing.

That afternoon, as I was grabbing my bag to go home, Adrian pulled me aside. A couple of Grade Eight boys walked past kissing the inside of their elbows at us. I rolled my eyes. What was it about some boys that they insisted on being so immature?

'I've been thinking about it,' Adrian said.

My heart leapt and jolted my face into a smile. 'You'll come?'

'I'll make a deal with you. I'll go on a day trip to Movie World with a bunch of people I don't know, other than you.' I clapped my hands and did a little bounce up and down. He lowered his voice and moved in close to my ear. 'If you'll admit the truth about the alcohol at school saga to Uncle Steve before the end of the term.'

I frowned. 'Why? What difference does it make?'

'It always makes a difference, Miss Kathleen Maree, because it means you don't have anything to hide anymore.'

I screwed my face up. 'That's not a fair deal.'

'Yes, it is. You face your fear and I'll face mine.'

I took a deep breath and nodded. 'Fine. Sure. I'm gonna do it, you know. Then you'll have to come to Movie World—no excuses—okay?'

Adrian swung his bag up onto his back and raised his eyebrows at me. As he walked off down the hall, he raised his hand and put his thumb in the air. I took that to mean a yes.

***

On Thursday afternoon, as soon as the bell rang, I picked up my bag and headed for Principal Dean's office. Although the corridor was full of excited kids talking about how tomorrow was the last day of Term Three, I was focused on one thing and one thing only: the consequences of going back to Mr Dean to tell the truth.

Mr Dean's office door held a plaque that simply read 'Principal' in silver. I tapped lightly on the door, hoping that Mr Dean wouldn't be in there. That way, I could just tell Adrian that I'd tried. But no such luck. Mr Dean opened his office door and with a surprised look on his face, said, 'Kat! Good to see you. Come on in.'

I walked into the room and sat in the same chair that I'd sat in almost six weeks ago.

'Thanks for seeing me, Mr Dean.' I wished I could have crawled under the desk and spoken to him from there. That might have been easier. But I needed to face up to this and tell it like it was, face to face, student to principal. If only my head and mouth would cooperate.

'What can I do for you, Kathleen? You must be relieved for the end of the term, and you're officially free from lunchtime detentions.'

'Yes, sir. Though they haven't been all that bad. In fact, I've kinda liked having something to do. It has helped having Adrian in there with me.'

'You have made a big difference in his life, Kat. He's been a different boy since the two of you became friends. I was worried about him for a while there. And I do like it when I can see a student making the most out of a bad situation, as you have done.'

I smiled weakly. 'But there is something I need to tell you, Mr Dean. About that whole alcohol-at-school thing.'

Mr Dean sat down at his desk and put the end of his pen in his mouth. 'Go on.'

'Well, you see. I didn't exactly tell you the truth that day...

about the alcohol.'

Mr Dean looked at me with a frown. His eyebrows joined at the middle when he pulled that face. 'I'm all ears.'

I told Mr Dean the whole truth, the whole story—right from Paige meeting me at the school gate that morning bragging she'd brought something special to share with us at recess, right up to the moment Mr Wally stopped to offer his farewells to Megan.

'So, the four of us sat out the front of your office and decided that I should take the blame. Keira was scared her mum would completely flip out, Paige figured you'd expel her for sure, and with Megan starting at her new school, she was worried she might lose her scholarship.'

'So, you said you'd take the blame,' Mr Dean said.

'I wasn't happy about it, for sure. But Paige has a lot of stuff going on in her life at the moment and I don't really know what it is exactly, but I think it would have been really bad for her if she'd been expelled. I couldn't let that happen to her.'

Mr Dean sat and rubbed his chin. 'Mrs Anderson tells me you and Paige aren't hanging around each other anymore. Is this why you're here? To exact some kind of revenge?'

'No way!' I sat forward in my seat. 'In fact, the opposite. I've paid for the crime, no one needs to get into trouble again. I just didn't want to keep the lie going. You don't need to punish Paige—I did her punishment. She doesn't even need to know that you know. I just wanted to tell the truth at last, that's all. Paige doesn't mean to do the stupid stuff she does. She just doesn't think, that's all.'

Mr Dean nodded again. 'Alright, Kat. Thank you for telling me the truth, though I wish you'd done it sooner. I'm not sure that Paige really appreciated what a good friend she had in you.'

I stood and Mr Dean came over to shake my hand.

'Thanks for understanding,' I said. 'You won't do anything

to Paige, will you?'

Mr Dean shook his head. 'No, I don't think so. I will have a chat to her next term about a few things, but we'll keep this particular truth between us for now. I assume you will tell your parents yourself?'

I nodded.

'Good.' Mr Dean smiled widely, so all his teeth were showing. 'See you at church on Sunday?'

'I'm hoping to see Adrian there, too, this time.'

Mr Dean raised his eyebrows.

'I've been trying to get him to come to church. I reckon this Sunday he just might.'

Mr Dean smiled again. 'Thank you, Kat. That means a lot to me.'

I left Mr Dean's office feeling like I was flying free, ready for the holidays. I knew telling Mum and Dad was going to be tough, but having told Mr Dean made me feel more confident.

As I left the school building to find Mum's car in the parking lot, I saw Adrian. He had his hoodie right up over his head so you could hardly even see his fringe. 'Hey, Fred,' I called out. He looked up at me, a frown on his face. 'See you Sunday,' I smiled. 'You better be there to meet my family before coming to the Gold Coast with us.'

He rolled his eyes. 'You didn't,' he called out.

'I did. Ask him tonight.'

He blew me a kiss. I poked my tongue out.

***

There was no time to tell Mum and Dad about the truth that night. I had bigger things on my mind. With the last day of term upon me, I wanted to do something special for Adrian, to mark the completion of our lunchtime detentions together.

I had already decided what I wanted to do. We'd gone to so many amazing places during our times in detention. This time, I wanted to take him somewhere.

At first, I was thinking Disneyland in California. But then I realised that we only ever went to places in the United States. It was time for a change of country.

I had wanted to visit Paris ever since I saw a documentary on the city in Grade Five. It seemed the perfect time and place to visit. But I needed to do some research first. So, with a pen, paper, my school Atlas opened to the page about France and permission for an hour and a half of computer use, I got stuck into planning tomorrow's trip.

CHAPTER 16

'I've got a surprise for you at lunch,' I said to Adrian in English. I was working on a short story piece I was supposed to have finished already. He was drawing, of course.

'What is it?' Adrian asked without lifting his eyes.

'I'm not going to tell you. That's the point of a surprise.'

Adrian grunted.

'But you have to meet me in the tunnel at second lunch, okay?'

He looked up briefly. 'What else would I do with my lunchtime?'

I smiled. I could think of a couple of things Adrian used to do with his lunchtimes, like spending the whole time in Mr Dean's office. So much had changed in six weeks. I was happier at school now than I had been in a long time, even before Megan had left. And I knew Adrian was a big part of that.

I sat in the concrete tunnel and ate my chicken in silence. Adrian had said he'd be a little late, as he had something he needed to do first. I had committed most of my notes on France to memory, but I pulled the printed sheets out of my pocket and glanced over the plan one more time.

I was bursting with excitement by the time Adrian got to the tunnel and positioned himself next to me. As he sat down, I took his hands.

'Have you eaten lunch already?'

'Yes,' Adrian said.

'Then are you right to go?'

'Go where?'

'I'm taking you to Paris,' I said.

Adrian frowned and looked surprised. 'You want to go to France? This is your surprise for me?'

I nodded enthusiastically. 'Come on, we've heaps to do. We don't want to be late.'

'I don't know Miss Kathleen—' Adrian started.

'I won't take no for an answer. Come on, close your eyes with me. The walls of the tunnel are breaking down and falling around us. The concrete under our feet is flattening out and—can you smell that? Pastries and buttered croissants—we're on a street corner in Paris.'

I described the giant steel and glass pyramid looming before us, and the massive old buildings that looked like golden palaces that lined either side.

'Where are we?' Adrian asked.

'We're standing at the entrance to Le Louvre.'

'What's Le Louvre?'

'It's an underground museum. Come on, let's go inside.'

'What? Wait, underground?'

'Yes. That okay?'

'Sure. Underground is fine. It's just, why do we need to go underground?' I could feel his hand tightening around mine again.

'This just takes us down to the lobby. Then we'll come back up, into the buildings. There is something here in particular that I want to show you.'

We walked into the pyramid and down the spiraling staircase. Light reflected down through the glass pyramid over us and onto the railing and silver pillions. We walked alongside crowds of people standing and pointing, or reading information sheets. Some people were just standing around chatting and others stared at faceless statues as though it was someone they had once known.

'Here, this way,' I said and lead Adrian to the beginning of a long corridor.

The hallway was covered with wall-to-wall paintings, some as tall as the ceiling and as wide again. The arched roof was all glass—a giant, continuous sky. Many of the paintings were wrapped in antique gold frames, as if they were as much a part of the artwork as the paintings. Other paintings stood on their own merit. Kings or princes of days gone by stared down at us.

'There are a lot of paintings of Mary in here,' Adrian said. 'Look, this one has a halo over her head.'

'Wow, a halo, huh,' I said. 'Well, she was the mother of God.'

'I wonder why they make such a big deal out of her?' Adrian asked.

'Maybe because deep inside we're all jealous that she was chosen for such an amazing job, and we weren't.'

'Ya think?' Adrian said. 'Bringing up God? I wouldn't have wanted that job. I reckon it'd be hard enough having a normal kid.'

I thought about George. 'Yeah, I guess so. But at least you wouldn't have to worry about sending him to the time-out corner.'

Something flickered across Adrian's eyes—was it fear? Then he chuckled.

A bit further ahead, a crowd had gathered.

'Oh, this must be it. The thing I brought you here for.'

'What is it?' Adrian asked.

'Oh, you know. Just a little painting we like to call the Mona Lisa.'

We broke through to the front of the crowd, and there she hung on the wall in a chunky golden frame.

'It's smaller than I expected,' I said. 'Though I guess it might just look small because she is hanging alone on such an enormous wall.'

There was a sheet of glass in front of the painting and it was roped off so we couldn't get close to it.

Yet still, Adrian was transfixed.

'Do you like it?'

Adrian nodded. 'It's beautiful. Look at the way her hand rests so gently across her arm. The hand that is curved around the chair's arm could be real. I wish I could see it without the glass in front of it. I wonder how it feels, if it's smooth or if the paints left it rough and bumpy.'

I shrugged. 'I don't know, sorry.'

We stood in silence, just looking at her.

'You know, you could do this one day,' I whispered.

'What, come to Le Louvre?'

'No, draw. Paint, like this. Create artwork that people stand and stare at, that people queue for ages to catch a glimpse of. You could do this. Your drawings are amazing. You have this kind of talent, you know.'

A puff of breath escaped Adrian's mouth, pushing his lips out, making a slight sound.

'Come on, let's go home,' Adrian said.

'Wait, not yet! I haven't taken you to the Catacombs,' I said. 'It's one of the have-to-go places when in Paris. We can skip the Eiffel Tower, but not the Catacombs—please!'

Adrian looked doubtful.

'It won't take long. Just a quick look.'

He nodded.

The walls of Le Louvre fell away around us and we were

standing on a quiet street. A small dark green building with a pointed roof was in front of us. The white flowers in bloom on the bush beside it smelled sweet.

'Here we are, this is where we go in. Come on.'

We walked through the small green door and down a dark stairwell lit with artificial lighting.

'I'm not sure about this, Miss Kathleen. Why are we the only ones here?' Adrian asked.

'I don't know,' I said. 'It's a popular tourist attraction. There are usually lots of people in these sorts of places.'

The walls appeared damp, but when I ran my hand along them, I felt dry mud and stone. I could hear Adrian's breathing quicken.

'There isn't much lighting and it is very cramped in here,' Adrian said. 'I don't like it, Kat. I don't like it.'

'Just a bit further. It's okay,' I said. 'Just around this bend. Here we go, look, we're in the first corridor.'

We entered a room lined from ground to ceiling with bones and skulls. They were stacked up on each other like a giant jigsaw puzzle, each bone fitting in a precise location within the wall.

'It's an old mine, but the people of Paris ran out of room in their cemeteries, so they dug up the old bones of people and put them in here. There's like six million people buried in here, under the city.'

Adrian squeezed my hand, and then again so tight it hurt.

'Ow, you're hurting me,' I said. I looked at Adrian in the dim light and could see he had his eyes squeezed shut tightly. 'What's the matter? Adrian?'

But Adrian just stood there as if he were frozen, his hand glued to mine, his eyes squished and his breathing shallow. 'Adrian,' I said a bit more forcefully. I shook him with my free hand. 'Adrian.' I leaned in closely. He wasn't breathing!

'Adrian!' I yelled.

I opened my eyes and found myself back at school. I grabbed Adrian's shoulder again and shook him. His eyes were still shut tightly and he was still holding his breath.

'Adrian!' I yelled again.

This time he opened his eyes, but they were blank and lifeless.

'Are you okay?' I could hear the bell ringing in the distance. 'Adrian, are you okay?'

He looked at me for the briefest moment, before crawling out of the tunnel and running. I took off after him, but he was much faster.

'Adrian!' I called out. 'I'm sorry! Adrian, what did I do?' But he didn't stop, whether he heard me or not. Some of the Grade Seven boys were snickering at me. I glared at them. 'What are you looking at?'

'Somethin' ugly,' the shortest of the boys said. They all laughed and then took off towards their classroom. I shook my head. They were just stupid little kids. Like Adrian had said, not worth my time or energy.

'What's the matter, Mary?' I turned to see Paige and Keira walking towards me. 'Trouble in lovers' land? Oh, you poor baby. Now what will you do? I think the school is all out of dweebs for you to befriend.'

Paige still had a cigarette butt in her hand, smoke drifting carefree out one end. She held it up, closer to my face. 'Oh honey, what's the matter? Has mummy's little angel caught someone participating in a banned activity? Hmmm, what shall you do, Mary? What shall you do?'

I pushed her hand away from my face. 'You know it's really bad for you, Paige. You're going to get yourself into trouble even if no one dobs you in.'

Paige flicked the butt towards my face. 'Well, let's hope so. There's nothing I want more than to be expelled. Then, I can spend my time doing something other than listening to stupid teachers rattle on about stupid stuff I'm never gonna need to know.'

I looked at Keira, who just looked sad and shrugged. I felt sorry for Keira—Paige's only friend, the only person whom she had left in her life to confide in. Keira probably felt she had no choice but to follow along after her. I shivered, so glad to not be in that situation anymore.

I returned to class and took my seat up the back. Adrian's pencils and a half-finished picture of a woman with long flowing hair sat on his desk. I wondered if it was another picture of his mother. Adrian was not in class to ask.

CHAPTER 17

Adrian didn't come back to math class that day. And when I headed for Mum's car at the final bell, he was still nowhere to be seen. It was the last day of term and not only had Adrian run off, but he hadn't come out to say goodbye. I didn't like how much we seemed to hurt each other, how we seemed to end up fighting—when most of the time I didn't understand why.

That night I went to bed early, despite it being the first night of school holidays. I was wrecked. But I didn't sleep for very long. The remnants of a dream—more a feeling than any picture or story I could remember—caused me to stir.

I must have lay awake for half an hour, my heart heavy in my chest and my hands clammy. I kept replaying the trip to France over in my mind, wondering what I had said to make Adrian freak out the way he did. But I couldn't—nothing made any sense.

My slightly open window was allowing a breeze to waft into my room. It was the kind of breeze that suggested a change in season: the end of winter and the start of something new. I loved this time of year.

I listened to the rhythmic tap of nature against my window. Closing my eyes, I focused on the sounds, until the tapping became louder and...musical. I swear it was playing *The Music*

Box Dancer. It made me sit up in bed, wide awake. There was someone—or something—tapping on my bedroom window.

I felt around under my bed for something that could act as a weapon in the dark, and pulled out an old netball trophy. It was better than nothing. Channeling my Katniss Everdeen courage, I clasped the trophy firmly in my hand and walked over to the window. I turned my fish tank light off so I would be able to see outside and slowly pulled the curtains back from the window.

A dark figure stood there. The figure was at least as tall as me, but broad-shouldered. I drew breath to scream when I noticed the outline of a hoodie over the intruder's head.

'Adrian?'

I pulled the curtains open a little more. Sure enough, Adrian Jacobs was standing at my bedroom window. 'Are you crazy?' I whispered. 'What are you doing? I could have screamed. Or *killed* you.'

'What, with your netball trophy?'

I looked at the trophy in my hand; it did look pretty pathetic. 'If I got a good swing, I could have done some serious damage. Maybe.'

'Can I come in, Miss Kathleen Maree?' His voice was quieter than normal, and deeper.

'You want to come into my bedroom—now?'

'Please. I need to tell you something.'

I pulled the window back as far as I could. 'I guess so, but what on earth do you have to tell me that you can't tell me on the phone tomorrow?'

Adrian climbed in through the window. He took the trophy from my hand. 'I didn't know you played netball.'

'Used to,' I said, my hands on my hips. 'Until it got too expensive. But, I'm guessing you didn't come here to ask me about my sporting achievements, or lack thereof?'

When no explanation was forthcoming, I walked over and closed my bedroom door.

If Mum or Dad were to walk into the room right now, I could kiss goodbye any dreams of going to St Andrew's. 'Okay, Fred. Out with it. What are you doing here in the middle of the night?'

'I'm sorry, Miss Kathleen Maree, but I had to see you. I felt really bad about this afternoon, about how I ran off and then skipped class. I didn't even come out to say goodbye to you.'

'I did notice.' I sat down on the edge of my bed. 'So, what happened?'

Adrian sat beside me. 'I got really freaked out.'

'No kidding. But I can't figure out why.'

Adrian shook his head. 'It was the dark and cramped space.'

'I thought it was interesting that they have something like that under such a huge city, like Paris.'

'Have you noticed the places I take you have always been in the States?'

'Yeah, that was why I wanted to take you somewhere else. Somewhere new.'

'But there is a reason I always go to America.' Adrian clasped his hands together in his lap. He looked nervous. 'I've never told anyone this before, Kat.'

'Told anyone what?'

'My dad, when he was killed, he was on a business trip in New York.'

'That's awful.'

Adrian nodded. 'Before Dad left, I remember being really sad. I hadn't wanted him to go. Dad told me that every night while he was gone, he'd visit me in my dreams.'

I brushed some of his fringe out of his face, but he shook it back down.

'When he first died, I used to dream about Dad all the time. Sometimes they were good dreams, sometimes…not so good. But I never cared if they were good or bad because it meant I got to see him. But as I grew older, well, he stopped visiting my dreams.'

'So, what? Now you go looking for him?'

'I figured if I looked around enough, went to enough places, that one day I'd find him. And then we'll go find Mum, and she'll be okay again.'

I cupped his face with my hand and wiped the dampness on his cheek with my thumb. Fear and anxiety about my own dad's heart attack revisited me; my chest tightened as I struggled to breathe normally, imagining what it would have been like if he'd died that day.

Adrian put his arms around me and we sat in an awkward embrace for what seemed like forever. It was Adrian who broke the silence. 'Pretty messed up, aren't I?'

'I think it's beautiful.' He smiled at me, but his blue eyes were sad. 'I still don't understand your reaction in the Catacombs.'

'That's a bit harder to explain.' He sighed. 'Remember how I told you Mum got a boyfriend a few years after Dad died? His name's Michael. Mum was really depressed, and he came into her life saying that he was going to save us, to save Mum, and that everything was going to be okay from now on.'

I looked at Adrian puzzled. I knew this guy hadn't done anything like that.

'Well, his answer to fixing Mum's depression was to fill her with alcohol. Just light stuff to start with, after I'd gone to bed. I'd hear them talking. He'd say, "Just one more, it'll numb the pain, make you feel better". But it wasn't long before he had her drinking more and more, during the day, to bury the pain.'

'And you and your brother?'

'Michael didn't have time for Tom or me. At first, he just

kind of ignored us, hoping we'd go away, I guess. The more full-up on drink Mum got, the less she was able to look after us. Michael would just give Tom money and tell him to take me to buy something to eat.'

'That's terrible.'

'Tom was only fourteen at the time. He didn't know what he was doing. We'd go and buy some takeaway food. Sometimes only chips if Michael didn't give us much money. We didn't eat properly for years, until Uncle Steve found out about what was going on. He came for a surprise visit and called the police. But they couldn't find anything to charge Michael with, until they found out about what he'd been doing to me.'

'Why, what had he been doing?' As soon as the words left my mouth, I shuddered, not knowing if I wanted to hear the answer.

'Michael put up with Tom, but he hated me. He'd beat me for no reason. And sometimes he'd lock me in the bathroom and not let me out for days.'

'What? How could he do that?'

Adrian put his head down. 'He stunk of beer and smoke all the time, and sometimes he and Mum would go for days without eating. Tom got sick of it all and moved out, and that's when Michael started to get real angry at me, even when I didn't do anything wrong.' Adrian pulled his hoodie back off his head and began to undo the zip. 'Mum was getting real thin and pale. But when I said something about it, that's when he did this.' Adrian lowered his hoodie off his shoulders to reveal eight black circles and a couple of long, pink scars across the back of his neck. They looked like a tattoo that had gone horribly wrong.

'Michael did that to you?'

'The circles are cigarette burns. The gashes are from when he took to my hair with a kitchen knife; he wasn't a very good aim.' Adrian ran his finger along the scars perfectly, even though he had no way of seeing them. 'Michael hated my long hair 'cause Mum used to always say how much I looked like Dad with it. He'd grab my hair and cut it off with a kitchen knife, laughing if he missed and sliced my skin. He thought it was especially funny if I yelled out, so I learnt to bury the pain and stay quiet.'

I ran my fingers over the marks across his shoulder blades and neck. The black circles were smooth, but the long thin scars were bumpy.

'Why didn't you say something? Tell a teacher or someone?'

'Michael used to tell me that if I ever said anything against him, that he'd kill Mum. I believed him. I still do.'

'But Michael is in jail, now, yeah?'

'Yeah, he's in jail. When they realised what he'd been doing to me, they locked him up. But I had to tell them it was Michael who'd done it to me. I had to tell them the whole story. Mum was a mess. Tom refused to have anything to do with any of it.'

'Wow, Adrian. That's so heavy.'

He sighed. 'Mum begged them to let her keep me. They weren't going to at first. That's when Uncle Steve stepped in and said he'd keep an eye on us.'

'What about Tom?'

'Tom was seventeen by the time Michael went to jail. He'd gone to live in Brisbane.'

'So Mr Dean came and got you after that?'

'He came to visit us one weekend about two months after Michael went to jail. Mum was going through one of her paranoid phases over Tom's whereabouts and spending heaps of money on phone calls trying to find where he was living. There was no food in the house and I hadn't been to school for weeks. I didn't want to go with Uncle Steve, but he convinced me that if I stayed with Mum, she would lose custody of me.'

I whispered, 'So that's why you always wear a hoodie?'

'Yeah, I'm trying to grow my hair so it covers the scars, then I can stop wearing it once it's all covered up. I don't like wearing the hoodie because it was Michael who used to make me wear it all the time, so no one would see the marks.'

'Why is it taking so long for your hair to grow?'

'Michael used to shave my head—with hair clippers when he was in a good mood.'

'Adrian, I'm so sorry. That is the most horrible thing I have ever heard.' Adrian's face had hardened. He looked cold and unemotional, like he was telling the story about someone else, someone he didn't care about.

'Anyway,' Adrian said, 'that's what I wanted to tell you, so you'll understand what happened today, and why I have to go back to my mum. I can't leave her alone for too much longer—Michael's jail sentence wasn't that long. I'm sorry it isn't a nice story to go to sleep to.'

'Thanks for telling me. I'm sorry for scaring you today.'

'It's okay. I'll sleep better now. I hope you do, too.' He went to my bedroom window and climbed out. I watched his silhouette disappear into the darkness.

CHAPTER 18

When I woke the next morning, my first thought was Adrian's visit from the night before. I had to think it through. At first, I wasn't sure if it was a dream or if he really had visited me during the night, with nightmare-quality stories to share. But my netball trophy still sat on the corner of my desk, evidence that his visit had been real.

Thinking about Adrian and all that he had been through wasn't easy. Although it explained some things, like why he wore that hoodie all the time even when it wasn't that cold, I couldn't help but think I'd rather not know. It was easier to think things like that didn't happen in real life.

I grabbed my dressing gown and headed for the kitchen, where Dad was mixing the batter for Saturday morning pancakes. I kissed George on the top of his head.

'Morning, gorgeous,' Dad said. 'Happy first day of the holidays.'

I smiled. 'Thanks.'

'So, how are you going to spend your first day of freedom?'

I frowned—and then it hit me: no more grounding! 'Can I ring Megan?'

Dad laughed. 'Of course. After breakfast. George wouldn't let me cook the pancakes until you were up. He wants to eat them with you.'

'Yeah, and I starffin," George said.

I shot Dad a questioning look.

'Oh, come on Kat. That's an easy one. He means starving.'

I laughed. 'Oh, of course. Sorry, Georgie.'

As soon as breakfast was done, I brought Megan's number up on the home phone and pressed 'Talk'. It seemed to ring forever before Megan answered the phone.

'Megan!' I almost cried, it was so good to hear her voice.

'Kat! How are you? How has school been without me? How's Paige? I've missed you!'

We both laughed, and began filling each other in on how school had been, what Megan knew about Paige from talking to Keira, and how she had heard I'd been spending a lot of time with a certain boy from school. 'Is this guy the one you were talking about with the imaginary trips?'

'Um, yeah,' I said. 'He's been in detention with me, and, well, it gets pretty lonely when you're in there so much.'

Megan laughed. 'And is it seriously that boy who wears the hoodie all the time? Didn't Keira reckon his family was in the Mafia or something?'

'They're not. And he's alright—he's great, actually. He's had some stuff happen in his life, some really bad stuff, but nothing to do with that sort of thing.'

'Yeah? That's good to know. You know, Keira called him your boyfriend.'

I sighed. 'I don't know about that. It's complicated.'

'Has he kissed you?'

'Maybe.'

'Maybe means yes!'

'Okay then, yes. Just once.'

'So, he is your boyfriend then.'

'I like him. A lot. And I want him to meet you.'

'When?'

'I've invited him to Movie World for my birthday. You're still able to come too, aren't you?'

'I can't wait. We organised our holiday around it. We're leaving this afternoon and are coming home a day early so I can go.'

'You're going away? I won't get to see you until my birthday?'

'We're going camping with the families of a couple of my friends from St Andrew's. It's no big deal to be cutting it a day short. I can't wait to see you. You'll have to come and sleepover one day in the second week, so you can tell me exactly what that kiss was like.'

'I don't know about that, but sure, I'd love to come over. I don't have much on.'

'Oh good, 'cause I've got heaps of stuff booked in already. I only have a couple of days that I'm not doing something or going somewhere with someone.' She laughed. 'My friends are a very social bunch at St Andrew's!'

As we said our goodbyes, there was a sense of change lingering in the air. Megan sounded different, spoke differently, and despite her telling me about her new life at St Andrew's, there was a whole new part of her I couldn't really know now. For the first time, I wondered whether we would be able to stay best friends going to different schools, and whether my following her to St Andrew's would change that.

I spent much of my free time over that first week thinking hard about which school I'd go to next year, now I had the choice between St Andrew's with Megan, or to stay at Central, possibly with Adrian.

I knew Adrian's mum was important to him, and rightly so. But that meant he wanted to go back to her, and didn't seem at all keen to stay at Central with me. I had been stressing over whether I should be even considering going to St Andrew's when that would leave Adrian at school without a friend—when all he was thinking about was how to get back to his mum.

The safe thing for him to do was to stay with the Deans, where he was out of danger. But I knew he would never forgive himself if something happened to his mum. If I encouraged him to stay and something did happen, what if he blamed me and hated me forever? I could deal with Adrian Jacobs being out there in the world, even if I never saw him again, but to know he was thinking bad thoughts about me—well, that was something I couldn't handle.

And then there was Megan, who was making heaps of friends at St Andrew's—the kind of friends I was sure Mum and Dad would fall over backwards to see me hanging around with. But was St Andrew's really the right school for me?

By the time we all headed to Movie World for my birthday, I'd made a decision about my decision. I'd choose what school I wanted to go to next year for me—not Adrian, not my parents, and not even because Megan was there. I would decide what was best for me.

The freedom that came with this decision was reflected in the amazingly fun day I had hanging out with my friends and family at Movie World. My birthday brought my worlds together. Adrian and Megan got to meet and hang out together—and although Megan admitted to struggling with the whole idea of my hanging out with a boy, by the end of the day she was starting to get it. She couldn't help but like him, she said, especially because of the way he looked out for me. George adored Adrian right from the start—helped, no doubt, by the Batman toy Adrian gave him from his old toy collection.

After the trip, my family started inviting Adrian over to

watch movies or have dinner with us. It was completely weird, but by the end of the second week of the holidays, he was over at my house practically every other day.

One afternoon, Adrian returned the favour and invited the family to the Deans' for lunch. Rebecca refused to go, unable to handle the idea of going to her school principal's house in the middle of the holidays. I didn't think it was so bad; I was just glad I'd come forward and told the truth about the alcohol to Mr Dean before the term had ended. It didn't feel awkward or anything around him anymore.

We'd ended up staying at the Deans' most of the afternoon. Adrian had said he had something important to discuss with me, but George wouldn't leave our side. I was desperate to know what he wanted to tell me.

Over the holidays Adrian and I had been working our way through watching all the latest Marvel movies, and another movie night would provide the chance to be alone for a while. But when I went to ask Dad if it would be okay for Adrian to come home with us, he was talking very seriously to someone on the phone. I could hear the stress in his voice as he paced around.

'Yes, Luke, we can certainly do that. Is there anything else?' Dad said into his phone.

I saw him wipe a tear from his eye. What was going on?

'Who's your dad talking to?' Adrian asked.

I shrugged. 'Luke someone.' I couldn't remember anyone in the church named Luke, other than Luke Murray, but he was only nine years old.

Dad hung up the phone and sat down with his head in his hands.

'Is everything okay, Dad?' I asked.

He looked up, surprised to see us. 'Oh, sorry, yes, everything is fine. Well, sort of. That was Luke Harrison.'

'Oh, is that Mrs Harrison from church's son?'

Dad nodded. 'His mum got a cancer diagnosis today and it's not looking good. Where's your mum?'

'I think she's cleaning up George. He had an accident with a bowl of ice cream.'

Dad nodded. 'Sounds about right.' He gave a half smile, but clearly other things were on his mind.

'Dad, can Adrian come back to our place and watch a movie, please?'

Dad nodded. 'Sure.' His eyes looked glazed.

'You okay, Dad?'

He nodded. 'Just get your mum, hey? We need to get going.'

When Mum got into the driver's side of the car, I thought it odd. Dad always drove when the two of them were in the car. But I thought nothing more of it and Adrian and I went on discussing which of the Marvel movies should be the next on our list to watch.

It was after dinner, while Mum was putting George to bed and Dad was busy on the phone in his study, that Adrian and I finally had a chance to talk.

'I've been wanting to ask you something for a while now, Miss Kathleen Maree. But I also don't want to ask it of you. I just—I don't know any other way to do it.' He played with the Marvel DVD case sitting on his lap. The disk was already in the player ready to go.

'To do what?'

'Well, you know how I have to get back to my mum?'

I nodded.

'I talked to Uncle Steve and Aunty Vicki about it. They said as soon as the school year finishes up, that we'll drive down and see her, make sure she is okay. And while we're there, we can suggest she come back to have Christmas with us in Fairview.'

'That sounds like a good plan,' I said.

'Yeah, it is. Except, I've heard from my caseworker, Carry. She is the one who helped me when I needed to talk about what Michael had been doing to me. She still rings me up from time to time to see how I'm doing, and she tells me how Mum is going and stuff too. She is the one who told me Mum had moved to a different town. She tells me the stuff Mum forgets to tell me.'

'She sounds nice.'

'Yeah she is. Last time I spoke to her she said Michael was due for parole soon. She said if he has been well behaved in jail and says the right things, that he could be released early. She reckons there is a good chance he will.'

'And you think that is going to happen before Christmas?'

'Christmas is still, what, two and a half months away? Chances are he'll be out by then. But Uncle Steve says he is too busy during the term. So, I'm thinking I need a Plan B.'

'Plan B?'

'Yeah, a plan in case I find out Michael is getting out of jail before Uncle Steve and I can get to Mum.' I could hear Rebecca moving around in the bathroom. I turned the DVD's loop music up a little louder.

'And what? You still think Michael will come after your mum once he's out of jail?'

Adrian nodded. 'I've got no reason to think otherwise.' I could barely hear him; his voice was so soft. 'The last time I saw him, he swore he would get his revenge. And that it wouldn't be me he'd be coming for.' He sniffed loudly. 'I have to get to her. I have to beat him to her.'

'Can't you just tell the police, or that caseworker lady, or even Mr Dean?'

'I've told them all at some point,' Adrian said. 'The police say it's not anything for me to be concerned about, or they need proof. All they're concerned about is keeping Michael away from me. They're not worried about Mum.'

I swallowed hard. 'What does your mum think?'

'She still thinks he loved her and won't hurt her. She screamed at me last time I suggested Michael was no good for her. I stopped telling her after that.'

My heart was racing and my fingers were shaking. I didn't want to ask the question, but I knew I had to. 'What do you want to ask me?'

'I need a plan, Miss Kathleen Maree,' Adrian said. 'I've hardly been out of New South Wales since I was four years old. I don't know Queensland at all, other than Fairview. You've travelled heaps, both in the car and on trains and stuff, with your family.'

'Well, yeah. But I'm not sure how much help—'

'You're the only one I can ask, Miss Kathleen, please. I didn't want to ask you; I didn't want you to get involved. But I need your help to get to Mum. I have no idea where the trains run, or how to get around once I get off the train.'

'There are always buses. And taxis, if you're really stuck.'

'See—that's what I need. Someone who can sit down with me and help me plan the trip. Will you help me? Please, Miss Kathleen Maree.'

I shook my head and tried to swallow, but my mouth had gone dry. I didn't want to get involved. *At all.* Mr Dean would be completely unimpressed if he found out I knew that Adrian was planning to run away, and I'd helped him. And if my parents knew I'd helped him, that would probably mean no St Andrew's next year. 'I can't help you, Adrian,' I said. 'I'm sorry. I think you should stay with Mr Dean and go back in December, like he's planning. I'm sure your mum will be fine until then.'

Adrian looked at me for a moment, then turned his head, picked up the remote and pressed Play—which was worse than if he had yelled at me.

CHAPTER 19

Adrian and I didn't speak the whole movie. He didn't even hold my hand. And when Dad came in saying it was time to take Adrian home, he'd just stood up and moved towards the door.

I slid into the backseat of the car; Adrian sat next to my dad in the front.

The ten minute car trip was an uncomfortable silence. Eventually, I decided to break it. 'Have you heard how Mrs Harrison is, Dad?'

He met my gaze through the rearview mirror. 'She's doing okay, thanks. She has faith and that is keeping her strong.'

I could hear Dad breathing. 'Are you okay, Dad?' He was clutching his jaw with one hand, the steering wheel with the other. I saw him shake his head. He indicated and began pulling over onto the edge of the road.

'Dad, what's the matter?'

Adrian grabbed the steering wheel as it slipped out of Dad's hand. The car hit the curb and bounced a little as it came to a stop. 'Dad!' From the back seat, I could see Dad's head was slumped and his eyes had closed. 'Adrian, have you got your phone?'

'Yes, but I don't have any credit, only data.'

'It doesn't matter, you can still call 000.'

Adrian pulled out his phone and unlocked it. 'Where are we?'

'I think that's Burch Ave,' I said. 'Hand me the phone. I'll be able to give better directions.'

I called 000 and asked for an ambulance. 'It's my dad,' I said. 'Please hurry. I don't think he's conscious. He's not responding to anything we're saying.'

'Maybe we should get him out of the car?' Adrian said.

I shook my head. 'They'll be here in a few minutes.' The lady on 000 was telling me to stay on the line. 'I need to call my mum and let her know what's going on,' I said to her. 'But I don't have any credit on my phone.' The lady said she'd call Mum for me, and asked me to try to get Dad to respond by tapping him on the hand or face gently. I did as she said and Dad started to come around. 'He's stirring, but he's dopey and still not responding properly. Can you call my mum now, please?'

'I can hear the ambulance,' Adrian said.

'Can you wave to it please? Let them know this is the car they're looking for?'

Adrian got out of the car and started jumping around. As the ambulance pulled up, Adrian ran over and began telling them what had happened while I patted Dad's hand begging him to stay awake.

I pleaded with the 000 lady to call Mum. 'It's okay, we've got her on the other line.'

Dad was being helped out of the car and onto a stretcher. 'Can I go with Dad in the ambulance?' I asked. No one replied.

There was so much happening: the lady on the phone was speaking to me, Adrian was talking to the paramedics with Dad, and one of them was speaking into some radio thing. I had to focus. I said to the lady on the phone, 'I don't know what to do. What's going to happen?'

'Kathleen, it's all okay,' she said calmly. 'You're going to go in the ambulance with your dad. Your mum has organised someone to take her to the hospital and she will call by and pick up Adrian on the way. He'll only need to wait with the car for a few minutes. It's all organised. You just go with your dad.'

I nodded dumbly, thanked the lady and hung up. Adrian was helping me up into the back of the ambulance, and his hand squeezed mine as he moved away and the doors were shut in front of me.

One of the paramedics was hooking Dad up to a machine. Everything was so cramped in the ambulance, but he moved around like he was in an Emergency ward. 'Your dad is doing well,' he said. 'He may not seem it to you right now, but he's responding well under the circumstances. Just hold his hand and let him know you're here.'

As the ambulance arrived at Emergency, Dad was beginning to answer questions like what his name was. The beeping heart monitor suggested everything was okay for the moment.

As I stood by his bed, memories of the last time I was in hospital came streaming back. Grandma had been staying with us at the time, and she'd taken us from school straight to the hospital. I remember being too impatient to wait for the elevator, and racing up the stairs to the third floor, only to have to wait for Rebecca and Grandma to meet me at the top anyway. We rounded the corner where Dad was standing in the hallway waiting for us. I'll never forget walking into the little room and seeing tiny baby George for the first time, wrapped in a yellow blanket in Mum's arms.

This hospital was different though. It was brighter, newer-looking and the doctors hadn't been running around like crazy, like they had when Dad had had his heart attack. A peace washed over me.

Mum raced in, followed by Rebecca carrying a sleepy George. As Mum bent over and kissed Dad, he gave her a smile.

'Adrian and Mr Dean are in the waiting room,' Mum said. As I went out to see them, Adrian came and wrapped his arms around me. I sunk into them as though I was suddenly aware of just how heavy my body was.

'Is everything okay?' Adrian asked. 'Your dad, is he alright?'

'I think so. They've got him hooked up to a heart machine and the doctor seemed to suggest everything was looking okay now. They want to find out why he collapsed and stuff, though, so I think we'll be a while yet.'

'Good to hear, Kat,' Mr Dean said. 'I might just pop in and have a chat to your mum for a minute.'

Adrian and I sat down on the chairs in the waiting room. 'Are you okay?' Adrian placed his hand on mine. 'That was pretty full-on for a while there.'

'I'm really tired and my head is still throbbing.' I tilted my head from side to side. 'Thanks so much for all you did. I'm so glad you were there. I didn't even have my phone on me—it was just as well you had yours! I don't know what I would have done if you hadn't been with me.'

'You were the amazing one. It was like you just went into "code emergency" and just did what needed to be done.'

'Well, maybe a team effort,' I said. 'But I began to lose it at the end. Thanks for coming to check that everything was okay.'

'Hey, I care about your dad and all, but I really just came to check on you.'

I smiled. 'Even though I said I couldn't help you?'

Adrian shrugged. 'I'm sorry for being weird about that. It just takes me time to process stuff. I shouldn't have ignored you like that.'

I nodded. 'It's been a big day. I can't believe it ended with Dad back in hospital. I wonder why it happened again. What's with that?'

'Your dad was pretty quiet at my place this afternoon.'

I nodded. 'Plus, he asked Mum to drive when we went home, which he hardly ever does.'

'And wasn't he having a stressful conversation on his phone when we were about to go back to your place?'

'Mrs Harrison. I'd forgotten, yeah. Dad really likes Mrs Harrison. She was one of his key support people when he first took on the role of pastor in the church.'

I shook my head. 'I can't imagine what it would be like to lose someone that close to you. I've never really known anyone who has died before.'

Adrian's silence beside me was thunderous.

'What's it like?' I asked.

'I was only young when Dad died,' he said. 'But I still wish he'd never gone on that stupid business trip to the U.S. He wasn't supposed to go on them anymore, because he wanted to stay home with Mum, Tom and me. If he hadn't gone, my life would be completely different. Mum wouldn't have gone into a black hole, Michael never would have been a part of our lives. It's awful living with that kind of regret. I hate it.' Adrian put his head down in his hands and rocked back and forth on the seat. I put my hand on his back and rubbed it. 'That's why I can't let anything happen to Mum.' Adrian's voice was muffled by his hands.

'If someone had stood in my way of trying to get to the hospital for Dad this evening, well, I wouldn't have given up until I knew he was safe.'

Adrian looked at me. 'So, you'll help?'

I nodded. 'Yes, I'll help you.'

CHAPTER 20

The following day, Adrian and I spread out on my bedroom floor with writing pads, an iPad, a laptop, a map of Queensland and a printed copy of the Tilt Train's timetable. George was wandering in and out of my room to play with some of my Schleich animals. Mum and Dad's voices drifted in from the kitchen, and Rebecca was clearly in her bedroom because I could feel, rather than hear, her music through the floorboards.

Coffee smells wafted through the house. This was a good sign that Dad was feeling better, since Dad was the only one who brewed coffee. The chest pain that landed him in hospital for the night hadn't been a problem with his heart, but some sort of anxiety attack. It had still demanded rest for Dad, and Mum had been making sure he'd been doing exactly that.

'First things first,' I said to Adrian. 'Have you got much money?'

'I have a bit,' he said. 'About sixty-five dollars in my bank. And maybe fifteen in my wallet.'

'Okay, well that's a start,' I said, with Dad's laptop on the floor in front of me. 'But I'm not sure how far it will get you on public transport. Whether it is train or bus, you're still looking at about sixty dollars just to get from here to Brisbane and back again.'

'That much?' Adrian said. 'Wow, that's heaps. I would have

thought going on the train would be cheaper than that.'

'Some trains cost more than others.'

Adrian shook his head. 'I wish I had some sort of idea about this kind of thing.'

'Well, this is the easy part. Once you get to Brisbane, you've somehow got to get down to Byron Bay.'

'She doesn't live in Byron anymore,' Adrian said. 'She moved to Chinderah a couple of months ago.'

'Where?'

I watched Adrian open Google Maps on Rebecca's iPad.

'Here,' he said, showing me a map of New South Wales. 'It's close to the Queensland border, not that far from Tweed Heads. Practically no one lives there. We used to go there for holidays after Dad died. Before Michael. I wonder if that's why she moved there.'

I typed in a search for transport from Brisbane to Chinderah and scanned the results. 'The train line doesn't go that way,' I said.

'Oh? What does that mean?'

'Bus might be the only option. You can go the whole way from Brisbane by bus in, like, three hours. There's a coach station in the middle of the town.'

'Three hours on a bus! How much would that cost?' Adrian asked.

'How much would what cost?' Mum asked, popping her head into my room.

'Oh, we just need to look up bus and train tickets for our assignment,' I said, my face warming with the heat of the lie. 'That's what we need the internet for.'

Mum nodded. 'Okay, well I have made some lunch if you want a break.'

'Can we have lunch in here?' I asked.

Mum frowned. 'What about the no-food-in-bedrooms rule?'

'Please, Mum. We've still got a lot of work to do.'

Adrian shut the laptop. 'You know, I think we could use the break.'

Mum smiled. 'Thanks, Adrian.' She frowned at me as she left the room.

Adrian sighed and picked up the train timetable. 'It sure would be easier if we had heaps of money.'

'I think we already do, when you think about how most people in the world live.'

'True,' Adrian said. He looked at me, his eyes soft, the blue especially bright against the whites of his eyes. 'I could so kiss you now.'

I dropped my eyes and giggled. 'My mum would kick you out if she heard you saying that in my bedroom.'

'True again.' Adrian ran his fingers down my arm and tickled my wrist. 'You are wise and beautiful, you know. If people saw your soul, they would discover what the meaning of true beauty is.' He smiled. 'I wish I had your point of view of the world. You're always seeing the good in people and in situations, always hoping for the best. I like that about you. Don't ever change that.'

My cheeks were still burning when Mum stuck her head back into the room. 'Are you two coming? Everyone else is waiting in the kitchen.' She looked at me. 'Is it hot in here, Kat?'

I shook my head and stifled a giggle. 'No, it's okay. I just said something embarrassing.'

Mum smiled. 'Well, it's nice to see you happy.' She left again.

'You do look awfully hot, Miss Kathleen Maree,' Adrian said. 'Shall I get you a cold drink or something?'

'Shut up.' I grabbed a nearby notepad and swatted Adrian on the head with it. He pretended to be hurt.

Adrian rolled onto his back, looked at the notepad that had prices jotted all over it, and groaned. 'How am I going to do this, Miss Kathleen Maree?'

'Can you ask Mr Dean for money?'

He shook his head. 'And tell him what? No, I don't want to involve him. Besides, he already does so much for me, letting me live there and everything.'

'Could your mum meet you somewhere so you don't have to travel so far?'

Adrian drew his shoulders up to his neck and held them there a moment. 'Maybe. She does have a car. But I don't know what condition it is in, or if she'd have the money for the petrol to drive very far. I'd rather not ask her if I can get away with it.'

'I have some birthday money left over. I was saving it to keep my phone in credit. But you can have it.'

Adrian smiled. 'Now I really want to kiss you.'

I dropped my eyes to the floor.

'But there is no way I am taking your birthday money, Miss Kathleen Maree.'

'We're running out of options,' I said.

'You know what we need?' Adrian asked.

'A miracle?'

'A swim,' Adrian said, rolling over to face me. 'To try to get some heat out of those cheeks of yours before they start melting the plastic on this laptop.' He put his finger on the laptop and pretended to burn himself.

I groaned.

'Come on, your shout,' he said, jumping to his feet. 'We'll have lunch, then I'll buy the drinks once we're there.'

Before I could argue with him, he grabbed my hand and pulled me to my feet. 'Thank you, Miss Kathleen Maree, for your help today. I am eternally indebted to you.'

***

It was two nights later when I was again woken by a tapping on my bedroom window. At first, I ignored it and tried to go back to sleep. But it became more rhythmic. *Adrian.*

I pulled back the curtain to see him standing with his face partially hidden behind a shrub. I opened my window.

'Adrian, what are you doing here? Are you okay?'

He nodded. Then shook his head. It was difficult to see his face with the light behind me, but I could tell he'd been crying. He climbed in through my bedroom window.

'What's going on?'

'Is it safe?' Adrian gestured towards my open bedroom door.

'I guess so. But this is still very risky.'

Adrian sat down in the corner of my room, his knees up around his chin while I closed my bedroom door. 'My social worker, Carry, rang earlier,' he said. 'I heard her talking to Uncle Steve. Michael has been granted parole and is going to be released any day now. She said they've applied for a restraining order so he can't come within a hundred metres of me as a condition of his release.'

'Are you scared?'

'Not for myself!' Adrian looked at me with desperation in his eyes. 'Don't you get it either, Miss Kathleen Maree?'

'I get that you're scared for your mum, and you're not worrying about yourself at all!'

'No one needs to be worrying about me! It's Mum. She's the one in danger. She's the one they should be warning. She's the one needing protection!'

'Well, can't you ring her?' I said. 'Tell her that she's in danger and she should come up here. With the money you have saved up, you could easily pay for her bus fare to here.'

'I've tried,' Adrian said. 'I've been trying to ring her ever since I found out about Michael's possible release. But her phone keeps saying it has been disconnected.'

'Does Mr Dean know how to get in contact with her?'

Adrian nodded. 'He does, but I'm only allowed to ring her at certain times and with him in the room. I'm not due to ring her again until Sunday.'

'But that's two days away! Won't he make an exception, if there is something serious like this happening?'

'He won't,' Adrian said. 'It was part of the rules they put in place when Uncle Steve became my guardian. He won't break the rules. I know it. And he doesn't think Mum is in any danger anyway. They are all just worrying about me—but it's Mum they need to worry about!'

'I know, I know.' I stroked Adrian's arm. 'Well, it's clear we have to do something. Should we go to the police?'

'Not me.' Adrian's face turned cold and emotionless. 'I'm not sitting around waiting for some phone call to say she's dead. I'm going to Chinderah to find her.'

'When?' A heavy weight fell into the bottom of my stomach.

'Now.'

'Now? You can't go now. How are you going to get there? Walk?'

'If I have to'—his teeth were gritted—'I'll walk, run, hitch-hike, whatever it takes.'

'You can't do that,' I said, my hands shaking. 'You can't leave in the middle of the night with no plan on how you're going to get there—it would take forever. Not to mention how dangerous it would be.'

Adrian crossed his arms and rested his head on his knees. He began to rock.

'I'll tell you what…' A thousand thoughts tore through my head within the seconds I had to think them. 'Give me until the morning. I'll make up a story for Mum and Dad, and come with you. The first train doesn't leave until nine-thirty tomorrow morning. I'll meet you at the shopping centre, out the front of the Target entrance at nine. Okay?'

Adrian shook his head. 'No, Miss Kathleen Maree. I can't let you do that. You can't get involved.'

'Right now, you don't have any other choice. And I'm not leaving you to get there on your own.'

'It might not be safe.'

'Then you shouldn't be going, either.'

'I'm going.'

'Then so am I. I will at least get you to Brisbane and put you on a bus from there to your mum's.'

Adrian nodded.

'Right. Good. Now go home and get a good sleep. Pack a backpack and include some snacks and stuff. If it works out, we could have you back here in Fairview, with your mum, by Sunday night.'

I shoved Adrian out the window and collapsed on the bed. What the heck had I gotten myself into now?

CHAPTER 21

The sound of birds chirping from my phone on my bedside table made me wake up the next morning. It was seven-thirty and much too early for me to be up and about on one of the few remaining school holiday mornings. My head already hurt. But the smell of pancakes wafting from the kitchen along with George's happy murmurings drew me out of my room and towards the kitchen.

'Morning, everyone,' I mumbled as I rubbed my eyes and stumbled onto one of the stools at the kitchen bench.

'Good morning, Kat,' Dad grinned. 'You're up early. And so you should be. It's a fabulous day outside.' He pointed to the window where white sun pushed its way through the glass to warm the floorboards beneath it. It was difficult to look at.

'I agreed to meet Adrian and Megan at the shops this morning,' I said, which wasn't a total lie. I had agreed to meet Adrian, at least. 'Something about a shopping crisis, and then Megan asked if I wanted to hang out at her place tonight. Could you or Mum drop me down the street around nine o'clock?'

'Is Megan's mum okay with all of that?' Dad asked. 'Maybe I should call her.'

'It's fine, Dad. This is Megan we're talking about. She always asks first.'

Dad nodded. 'True. Okay, and you're right for some money?'

'Yeah, I've still got my birthday money, so I have heaps. Thanks, Dad. I'll go get ready.'

I walked out of the kitchen and sighed heavily. I doubted I would have gotten away with all those lies if I'd told the same story to Mum. I shook my head and headed for the shower. I needed a good wash; the guilt was already starting to leave a slimy feeling on my skin.

Adrian was waiting when Dad pulled the car into the shopping centre parking lot, right on nine o'clock. His hoodie was pulled lower than usual and his hands were hidden within it. He had 'suspicious' written all over him.

'So, we'll see you later tonight, then?' Dad asked.

'Yeah,' I said, 'probably.' I pulled my black backpack out from the back seat.

'Probably?' Dad was eyeing off my backpack. 'What do you mean?'

Butterflies danced in my stomach. 'I brought a change of clothes just in case Megan asks me to stay over. You know, if we start watching a movie or something. That way, you guys won't have to drive out and pick me up late. I'll let you know, though, okay?'

Dad seemed satisfied with my lie. 'Have a great day, honey.'

I jumped out of the car, throwing an 'I love you' back at him, quite convinced I was going to get away with my little impromptu trip to Brisbane. Why was lying so much easier now?

'Are you okay?' I asked Adrian, as Dad pulled away. 'You don't look so good.'

'I'm alright.' He didn't stop looking at the ground. 'I'm not sure what I feel worse about. My lying to Uncle Steve after all he has done for me, or you lying to your parents for my sake. I'm really sorry, Miss Kathleen Maree.'

'It's okay. I didn't have to do this.'

'Really?' Adrian looked at me, the blueness of his eyes surrounded by red. Was it from crying or lack of sleep? 'I feel as though I didn't really leave you with any choice.'

'Of course you did. I'm here because you need me and that's what's important.'

'What did you tell your folks?'

'That I was hanging out with Megan after shopping. I also said I might end up staying over at her place, just in case I'm back really late or something.'

'But, then—'

'But that won't happen.' I smiled. 'Our day will run smoothly and I'll be home in time before any of the adults in my world become suspicious.'

'And Megan?'

'I sent her an email, but she hasn't responded yet. She'll be cool though. We can trust her. Anyway, if we miss this train, we're not going to get to Brisbane until mid-afternoon. Come on, let's go.'

With Dad well out of sight, we began walking towards the bridge that crossed over the railway tracks. The street was quiet, with some shops just opening their doors for the day. The smell of coffee brewing made my stomach gurgle. I wished I'd asked Dad to make me a coffee before we left.

'Miss Kathleen, what are we going to do once we're in Brisbane? How will I get to Chinderah from there?'

'I'm not exactly sure, yet. I put some extra data on my phone this morning so we can research while on the train.'

'I'm not sure I have enough money to catch a second train out of Brisbane, let alone a bus after that.'

'Let's just get on this train and we'll figure out the rest when we're there, okay?'

The train station smelled of cigarette smoke and there

were at least fifteen people already waiting on the platform. I opened the outside pocket of my backpack and pulled out my purse. My heart was racing. The man behind the glass panel looked at me suspiciously.

'Two one-way tickets to Brisbane, please.' I kept my eyes down as though I was looking for the right money.

'One way?' Adrian whispered. 'What about you getting back tonight?'

'I'll buy a ticket in Brisbane, once I know you're on your way to Chinderah safely and everything has gone to plan.'

The man behind the glass cleared his throat. 'Concession?'

I nodded.

'Have you got ID?' The man looked past me to Adrian.

Adrian shook his head. 'No? What do you mean?'

'Student ID, to prove you're a student.'

I swallowed hard and looked intently at Adrian. 'Did you bring your ID card? Remember Mum said you might need it.'

Adrian looked at me like I was from another planet. 'I, errr, must have forgotten it. I think it's, maybe, in my other shorts?'

The man behind the glass panel mumbled. 'Don't worry this time. But you need to carry your student ID if you want the discount. Remember that. I won't go so easy on you next time.'

Adrian handed me his half of the money and I paid the man, managing to keep my hands steady.

I shoved the tickets into my purse and moved closer to the train tracks. It was almost twenty past nine. I looked around for somewhere to sit, but was instead confronted with the surprised face of Mrs Harrison.

'Kat,' Mrs Harrison smiled. 'I thought it was you. What brings you here?'

My heart leapt into my throat while all hope of managing to get Adrian to Chinderah, without my parents' knowledge blew away with the morning's warm breeze. 'Mrs Harrison! I'm, ah, just heading out to do a bit of shopping with friends. The others must be running late.' I looked at my watch as though I was worried about the time. Man, I was getting good at this lying thing.

'Oh, that's lovely. Going to the markets at Eumundi, are you?'

'Probably,' I said, mentally fighting the heat rising in my cheeks. 'We haven't really planned that much ahead. We just wanted to get out of Fairview for the day.'

'It's so good to have time out with friends, especially at your age. You are growing up.' Mrs Harrison had such a sweet face. It was a shame she was so unwell.

'Mum and Dad told me about, the, ah...' I said, heat rising up into my face.

'It's okay, dear.' Mrs Harrison's eyes wrinkled in the corners. 'It's just cancer. And who knows, I may beat it again yet.'

I nodded. 'I hope so.'

'Well, enjoy your day, won't you?' Mrs Harrison smiled and began walking back to her seat.

'Thanks. Ah, Mrs Harrison?' She turned back around. 'I didn't ask you what your plans for the day are.'

'I'm helping a friend celebrate her seventieth birthday tonight. And on Monday I've a quick trip to the hospital to see my specialist.'

'So, you're going to Brisbane?'

'Yes, I am. Why do you ask?'

'Oh, I was just going to ask if you wanted to have lunch with us, if we were going to the same place.'

'That's very kind of you, Kathleen. Thank you.'

Adrian and I headed down the platform to where the train would stop. I breathed out long and hard, relieved to not be able to see Mrs Harrison anymore.

'Wow, that was full-on,' Adrian said.

I nodded. My heart was still beating so fast that I was having trouble calming myself.

'You could have won an Oscar for that.'

'Ha ha. You do realise I just told another whopping great lie to one of the sweetest ladies in the whole of Fairview.'

'Sorry,' Adrian said. 'Again.'

'That's okay. But it is going to complicate things. She's, like, super close to my parents and I just suggested we were getting off at the Sunshine Coast, but we are both getting off at Brisbane. We'll have to make sure we don't let her see us.'

'I thought you were vague enough. Besides, we could be shopping for the day in Brisbane.'

'Fairview to Brisbane and back in one day, just for shopping? Not really a plausible story. Best if she doesn't see us once we're on the train.'

'What was the whole thing about asking her to have lunch with us?'

I shrugged. 'I needed a reason to ask her where she was going today.'

Adrian smiled. 'You're amazing.'

'What,' I said. 'An amazing liar?'

There was a whistle and the rumbling of the tracks told us our train was approaching. I held back, looking at my watch as if I were still waiting for our made-up companions on the platform, but really watching Mrs Harrison being helped onto the train. Once she was on, Adrian and I climbed aboard. 'This lying business is rotten,' I said as we made our way through the carriage. 'I can see now why people say it is so difficult to keep a lie. You have to remember so many things!'

Adrian smiled sweetly at me.

'Don't look so innocent, you.' I swatted him on the arm with my purse. 'Where should we sit?'

'I don't know, but not this carriage. It's too full already.' Adrian started to move off.

'Hang on. Just let me put my purse away first.' I threw my backpack onto a seat and opened the front pocket.

'You shouldn't put your purse in that pocket,' Adrian said. 'Someone could steal it out of there easily.'

'Is that right?' I chuckled.

'Why is that funny?' Adrian asked.

'Because you can't catch a train, or find your way around a city, but you know not to put a wallet in the outer pocket of a backpack because it might get stolen.' I closed the front pocket zip and slid my purse into the larger pocket.

'I guess you know what you know because your family takes you places, on trains and stuff. I know what I know because of the type of people my family hang around with.'

The train began moving away from the station as we moved into the next carriage. 'Let's just sit here,' I said, slipping into an empty row. The lady in the row before us was wearing strong perfume, making me sneeze. Then something caught my eye. I covered my face with my hands.

'What's the matter?' Adrian asked.

'At the very front of the carriage. The lady in the third seat. Take a look.'

Adrian stood a little, the movement of the train making him sway. 'I can't see anything. Just a couple of older ladies.'

'Yeah, *older ladies*. Look again. The one with the bun on her head—it's Mrs Harrison. I'm sure of it.'

CHAPTER 22

Adrian and I sat low in our chairs as I watched Mrs Harrison. Cane sugar fields flashed past us from outside our window.

'Okay, so we need to come up with a plan,' Adrian said.

'I just can't believe she is here, not only on the same train but in the same carriage. I'm going to get busted for sure.'

'Don't stress, Kat. She doesn't know we're here. She only knows we're on the train somewhere.'

'Yes, but if she does see us sitting back here, what is she going to say?' I said. 'I told her we were waiting for other friends. If she sees us alone, she'll know I was lying.'

'Okay, that's a point. But maybe they were just running late and missed the train.'

'I think the bigger problem is if she does see us, and she thinks we're getting off around the Sunshine Coast, but we need to stay on the train until Brisbane. Same as her.'

'Look, let's try working out what we're going to do after we get to Brisbane,' Adrian said. 'If Mrs Harrison sees us, then we'll decide what to do about her.'

With my phone in my hand, I opened the Safari browser and typed in 'bus from Brisbane to Chinderah'. 'Hey, this could be good. Greyhound does a bus trip for only nineteen dollars. Why didn't I see that last time we looked this information up!

Do you have enough money for that?'

'Yep,' Adrian said, pulling out his wallet. 'I still have almost forty dollars. I might be able to buy myself some dinner, too.'

I pulled out my purse. 'I have some money I can lend you if you need it anyway.' I looked at Adrian and smiled. 'We're gonna be able to do this.'

He took my hand and squeezed it.

'This is amazing,' Adrian said, looking out the train window. 'It's like being on a plane but on the ground.'

'Have you ever been on a plane?' I asked.

Adrian shook his head. 'My dad, he was really into planes when he was younger. One of the few memories I have of Dad, not long before he died, was when he took Tom and me to an air show. There were heaps of planes there, old ones and fighter jets. There was a passenger aircraft there that we could walk around inside. I remember Dad telling me about how he always tried to get a seat on the wing, because he reckoned it was the safest place to sit on a plane. I didn't think anything about it at the time, but I wonder if he was afraid of flying.'

'Did he fly very often?'

'He used to. His company sent him to the U.S. quite a lot. But he got sick of it; he wanted to spend more time at home with Mum and us. That's what Mum says anyway.'

I hung my head, fiddling with my fingers, not knowing what to say. I wished I could take all the pain away from him and make it my own. It didn't seem fair that he had gone through so much already in life.

We sat in silence. Adrian closed his eyes. I Googled Chinderah, but even Wikipedia didn't have much to say about the town. I forced my shoulders to relax. I'd been so stressed all day, but every moment that my phone didn't ring, was another moment that we had got away with our plan to get Adrian to his mum. If neither my parents, or Mr Dean, were ringing, then surely that meant they didn't know Adrian was on a train to New South Wales, with me in tow.

Adrian stirred then, rubbing his eyes with his fists

'Look. This is Cooroy station. The next station is Eumundi.' I could feel my shoulder muscles tighten.

'So?'

'This is around where we'd get off to go shopping. The markets Mrs Harrison mentioned are at Eumundi.'

'Has Mrs Harrison been sitting in her seat the entire trip?'

I nodded.

'Then she can't have seen us. I think we're safe to stay on the train for now, don't you?'

I nodded again. What other choice did we have, really?

I flicked my phone back to Safari to look at the bus schedule again. I wouldn't have minded wandering around the markets at Eumundi. I wanted to buy some new sunglasses and maybe a new pair of bathers. Though, after this weekend, I probably wouldn't be able to afford such things.

'Oh no,' I groaned. I couldn't believe what my phone was telling me. How did I not notice this earlier?

'What? What's the matter?' Adrian asked.

'The bus that goes from Brisbane to Chinderah goes three times a day, but they're at like eight and eleven in the morning, and then ten past twelve. We won't get there in time for you to meet the bus!'

'What time are we supposed to get to Brisbane on this train?'

'Not 'til about twelve. So, we'd have to jump off the train, run to the bus area where ever that is, buy your ticket and get you on the bus, all in ten minutes max—if we're lucky and if the train is on time.'

'So, there is a chance, then?'

I rolled my eyes. 'Don't go getting all positive on me. It's virtually impossible.'

'But not wholly impossible,' Adrian said.

'Whatever,' I said, looking back through the information, hoping there was something I had missed.

'What's she doing out of her seat?' Adrian whispered. 'Mrs Harrison—I think she looked right at me.'

'What?' I looked through the seats in front of me to where Mrs Harrison had been sitting and sure enough, her seat was empty.

This was it. We were going to be caught for sure!

'You don't think she'd have recognised me, do you?' Adrian was whispering. 'She probably hasn't seen you yet.'

I looked at Adrian with his hoodie pulled up over his head in what must have been close to 30-degree weather. There was every chance Mrs Harrison recognised him—he stood out everywhere he went. I tucked my head down into my shoulders and glared at my phone.

'I could kiss you,' Adrian said quietly. 'Just as she walks past. That's what they do in the movies to stop someone from recognising someone.'

'And what if she still recognises me? That would only make things worse!'

'Sorry, just trying to be helpful.'

My head was hurting and the fear of being caught was starting to overwhelm me—not only from running away like this, but with all the lies I'd told to make it possible.

'The train is slowing down. Come on, let's go.' I jumped out of my seat and grabbed Adrian's arm. If Mrs Harrison said anything as we left our seats, I didn't hear her. We went through to the next carriage. 'We're coming to a station. We'll pretend we're getting off here.'

'What station is it?' Adrian asked as we stood at the exit door in the next carriage.

'I don't know. Let's hope it's a big one, or Mrs Harrison will wonder why we're getting off here.'

'What does it matter if she sees us anyway?'

I glared at him. 'Because the more suspicious we look, the more lies I'm going to have to tell my parents to cover up this trip.'

'You could always just tell the truth,' Adrian said. I glared at him again. If I did that, my parents would never trust me again. And I could say goodbye to going to St Andrew's next year. I couldn't get caught doing this. I couldn't bear the look on my parents' faces if they knew I'd lied big-time to them again.

As the train slowed, Mrs Harrison came into the carriage. She locked eyes with me just as the train's doors began to open. I heard her call my name as I grabbed Adrian's arm and pulled him out of the train with me, onto the station platform. Without thinking, I headed towards the first thing that looked like an exit to the station. I didn't dare to turn around as I again heard Mrs Harrison call my name.

'What did you do that for?' Adrian pulled back out of my grip and stood still. The train rolled out of the station beside us.

'We were caught, Adrian. We had to get off the train.'

'Well that's great, isn't it? Where are we?'

I pointed to the station sign. 'Caboolture.'

Adrian hung his head. 'No way we'll make that connecting bus to Chinderah now.'

This wasn't the way the day was supposed to go. I'd been so wrapped up in not wanting to get caught, that I'd forgotten the purpose behind the trip. Adrian's mum was still in danger. And we were back to being stuck without a way to get Adrian to Chinderah.

CHAPTER 23

Adrian and I stood on the platform and watched the train Mrs Harrison was still on disappear down the tracks to Brisbane —the exact place we had wanted to go. I looked at my watch. It was after eleven and my stomach was rumbling, but a much greater problem loomed before us: we still had to find a way to get Adrian to Chinderah. I needed to think, and to think, I needed food.

I reached into my bag for a muesli bar. Beside me, Adrian's sunken shoulders told me I owed him an apology. There was every chance Michael was out of jail and heading for Adrian's mum, and I'd sacrificed getting there to protect my latest lie.

'I'm sorry for not being very nice to you on the train,' I said. 'I was pretty stressed.'

'You were. And I don't think we needed to get off the train. We could have hid in the toilets or something.'

I shrugged. 'I guess so. But I'm so relieved not to have Mrs Harrison around now. I'm sure we can work something out.'

'What do you suggest?'

I looked down at my backpack. 'I suggest we find somewhere to sit and eat and try to come up with a Plan B.'

'You mean Plan C?'

'Hmmm, could be more like Plan D even.'

Adrian picked up my backpack and we walked over the

pedestrian bridge to a small grassy area next to the station. 'Look,' Adrian said, pointing to a bus as it pulled into the station. 'Buses leave from this station too. Maybe we could ask about a bus to Chinderah?'

I nodded. 'Well, that one goes to Bridie Island, so it's no good to us. Let's eat first.'

'Can I look on your phone?' Adrian asked, taking a bite from his own muesli bar.

I handed it to him. He sat staring at the screen. His eyes were so sad, I had to keep reminding myself why we were here. The purpose of this trip wasn't to hide a bunch of lies from my parents. It was to rescue his mum.

'Find anything?'

'Yeah, I think so,' Adrian said. 'Have a look at this.'

I took the phone. 'Uber? Really?'

'It says it can get us to the city in thirty-five minutes.'

'Yeah, but look at the cost! Plus, we'd be getting into the car with a person we know nothing about.' I showed him the phone.

'It is a bit out of our price range, I guess.'

'But look at this,' I said, moving so I was sitting beside Adrian. 'You could catch the train to what looks like somewhere near Burleigh Heads, and then there are local bus services that go between there and Chinderah every couple of hours.'

'But how often do the trains leave Brisbane for Burleigh Heads?'

'I'll look it up.' I clicked the link. 'You'd go to a station called Varsity Lakes. And a train leaves Brisbane for that station every hour!'

Adrian jumped to his feet. 'Come on, let's go see when the next train leaves for the city.'

We headed back across the pedestrian crossing to the ticket box. Adrian asked a man in a business suit when the next train into the city was coming. 'Five minutes or so,' the man said.

'That's awesome,' Adrian said. 'We're back on track, Miss Kathleen Maree!'

I dug around in my backpack, unzipping each zip carefully, pulling bigger items out to find my purse.

'Adrian.' I could feel the blood draining from my cheeks. 'I can't find my purse.' I put my backpack down on the ground and knelt beside it, in order to get a better look through each of the three sections.

'When do you last remember having it?' Adrian asked.

'Um…' I thought for a moment. 'On the train. When you suggested I put it in a different pocket. I stopped to put it back in my backpack then. Before we got to our seats.'

I pulled pretty much everything out of my backpack. My purse was definitely not there.

'Maybe it fell out when you got your phone out?' Adrian suggested.

I nodded. 'Maybe. We got up in such a rush, perhaps I didn't notice. Adrian, what are we going to do now? It had our train tickets in there and everything.'

Adrian put his hand on mine. 'I'll talk to the ticket guy and see what he says. Maybe it won't matter if we don't have tickets on us. Then maybe we could report your purse missing once we get there. Someone might have handed it in. You never know.'

Adrian went over to the ticket box. My shoulders slumped.

There was a boy and girl, not that much older than us, kissing in the corner of the shelter. I watched the way the boy wrapped his hand around under her hair and held her face into his. I wondered what it felt like to kiss someone like that. The couple stopped kissing and the guy looked at me. He gave a creepy, crooked smile and called out, asking if I wanted to join in. I shuddered and went back to shoving everything back into my backpack. When I dared to look back a minute later, they were kissing each other again.

'You right?' Adrian asked.

'I guess so,' I said. 'Did you have to buy more tickets?'

Adrian moved his head, but it wasn't a nod, or a shake, to answer my question. 'Come on, the train is due any minute.'

I looked back to the boy and girl who had been kissing, only to see him open his eyes mid-kiss and wink at me. It made me feel a little bit sick.

'So, you didn't have to buy tickets?' I asked.

He smiled uneasily.

'You did?'

'I did. But it's okay. They didn't cost much.'

The train into the CBD wasn't anywhere near as nice as the tilt train we'd been on. I hadn't travelled on city trains before. All I could think about was my lost purse and all my birthday money in it. I knew Adrian didn't have a lot of money and doubted he would have enough to buy a bus ticket to Chinderah as well as a return ticket to Fairview for me. The hopelessness of the whole trip was growing on me. What had made us think we could even get him to Chinderah? And Adrian hadn't spoken to his mum for two weeks. It was still possible Adrian could get all the way and find she wasn't even there.

I leaned my head against Adrian's shoulder and closed my eyes. It wasn't very comfortable, like I'd assumed it was from couples in movies. Adrian's shoulder was bony and hard, but he sat still and let me rest while he looked out the window.

'We're almost there.' Adrian was shaking my shoulder gently. 'I think the next station is Brisbane Central.'

I stretched and rubbed where my head had been resting on Adrian. 'Did you sleep?'

Adrian shook his head. 'Too much to think about.'

‘Your mum?’

Adrian nodded again. ‘Mum and what I’ll find when I get to her.’

I took a drink from my water bottle and grabbed another muesli bar. ‘Guess I slept through lunch. Have you eaten?’

Adrian shrugged. ‘I’m not hungry. Let’s find Information and see about reporting your missing purse.’

We asked a lady at Information, but she said nothing had been handed in. She said to check again later today or tomorrow. I just wanted to go to sleep and wake up again at home.

As we walked away from Information, my head began to empty of any remaining optimism. ‘How much money have you got left?’

‘I dunno,’ Adrian said. He put his bag on the ground and sighed deeply. ‘Look, you wait here. Let me see if I can sort a few things out.’

He walked back to Information and talked to a young man for some time. Then he returned to where I was standing. He took my hand. ‘Okay, confession time. Miss Kathleen, I don’t have enough money.’

‘For what? What do you mean?’ The terminal was full of people rushing past, with no time to notice two distressed teenagers.

‘I can’t pay for you to get back to Fairview, let alone both of us. I hoped I might have enough to get us both to Chinderah, but the guy at Information said I don’t have enough for that either.’

A voice echoed out the arrival of a train that was stopping all station to Varsity Lakes. ‘So, you only have enough money for one of us to board this train?’

Adrian nodded.

‘I’ll stay here,’ I said. ‘You go to Chinderah and I’ll wait here in Brisbane for you and your mum to come and get me. Then we’ll go back to Fairview together.’

'Kathleen Maree,' Adrian said, his tone way too much like my mother for my liking. 'There is no way I am going to leave you in the middle of the city on your own. That is not an option.'

'But you can get to her then. You can tell her what happened to us and that will give her even more reason to leave Chinderah with you. And that way—'

Adrian put his hand up to my face. 'We are doing this together, or not at all. Separating is no longer an option. We either try to get to Chinderah, or we call Uncle Steve or your dad and ask them to come get us.'

'Do you think your mum would have driven us back to Fairview if we'd made it to her?'

Adrian shrugged. 'Maybe. I think it's still worth a try.'

I rubbed my arms, though they weren't cold. 'But how?'

'I have an idea,' Adrian said. 'It's a bit of a long shot. I don't know if it will work.'

'Okay,' I said, taking a deep breath. 'What is it?'

Adrian shook his head. 'I'll need to borrow your phone again. That okay?'

I frowned and handed over my phone, wondering what he was up to, and why he wouldn't tell me first. I watched him make a few phone calls, close enough to see his face but not to hear what he was saying. He was ringing, talking for a few minutes, hanging up and repeating. Until he had a slightly longer phone call, this one lasting a few minutes. His face was a strange mix of emotions: anger, sadness and hurt. He hung up the phone with what seemed a very frustrated push of the button.

'What was that all about?' I asked as I walked over to where he was standing. I could still see the anger on his face.

'Well, I have a plan,' Adrian said. 'Though it's not brilliant.'

'Well, what is it?' What on earth had made him so worked up in such a short period of time?

Adrian looked at me and sighed. 'Tom,' he said.

'Your brother?'

'Yeah. He lives in Brisbane.'

'So, you just rang him? Why haven't you called him before this?'

'Because today I had a reason to. A good reason. I didn't have his number—I had to ring around to find someone who had it. Between Mum being in danger and us being stuck in Brisbane, I had the reason.'

'And? What, is he coming to get us?'

Adrian sighed and wiped his fringe away from his eyes. His forehead was wet with perspiration and his hair was sticking to it. 'Not exactly. He suggested we catch a train out to him, and that once we were there, he'll talk about maybe helping us.'

'Did you tell him about your mum?'

'He won't listen. He doesn't care,' Adrian said, his eyes to the floor. 'That's why it has to be me to help her. No one else will. But Tom might help us, if we can get to him. He may not care about Mum, but I reckon he cares about what happens to me. It might be our best bet, and tickets will only be about four bucks, Tom reckons. What do you think?'

I shrugged. 'What other choice do we have?'

It looked like Adrian skipped a little as he headed back towards the ticket box. 'Goodna station, here we come.'

CHAPTER 24

By the time the train pulled into Goodna station, the sun had begun its journey down to the horizon and the air was cooling. The smell of jasmine reminded me of my nan's house, where the flower grew on an arched trestle in the garden, under which Rebecca and I used to pretend to get married.

'Are we waiting for someone here?' I asked. 'Is Tom meeting us?'

Adrian shrugged. 'It's a pretty dreary-looking station, don't you think?'

'Kind of grey, if that's what you mean,' I said. 'Did Tom say he would meet us here?'

Adrian shrugged again. 'Not exactly. But he did ask what time the train got in, so that's a good sign, isn't it?'

'Can Tom drive?'

'I doubt it,' Adrian said. 'I think you have to do a certain number of hours driving before you can go for your licence.'

'But someone could have been giving him lessons, now he's in Brisbane, yeah?'

'Maybe.'

We crossed the pedestrian bridge over the tracks and stood numbly in the carpark.

'Now what?' I asked, just as a small red car pulled into

the parking lot. A girl with cropped brown hair climbed out of the driver's side. She had a thin face and kind, gentle eyes. A boy got out of the other side. He looked like Adrian, but older, and without a hoodie.

'Brother,' the boy called out. As he reached where we stood, he embraced Adrian, slapping him so hard on the back that it made me wince.

'Tom,' Adrian said, his face red and awkward. 'This is'—he paused for a moment—'Kathleen.'

Tom looked me up and down, and smiled a big, goofy-looking grin. 'Aidy, you beast, you. What 'ave you been up to?'

Adrian shoved his brother in the shoulder. 'Shut up.'

The short-haired girl put her hand forward and smiled at Adrian. 'Harriet,' she said. She shook Adrian's hand and then mine. 'Good to meet you guys. Tom never told me he had a brother.'

Adrian rolled his eyes. 'No surprises there.'

'So, you guys are off to Tweed Heads or something?' Harriet asked.

'Chinderah,' I said. 'We've had a few problems along the way.'

'I'm going to see Mum,' Adrian said, looking sideways at his brother. 'But we're short on cash. Can you guys help us out?'

Tom ran his hand through his hair and tucked it behind his ears, but neither nodded or shook his head. Unlike Adrian's eyes, Tom's were dark and sunken, as though they had seen way too much. He looked at his brother like he both loved and hated Adrian being here.

'What'dya want?' Tom asked, pulling a wallet out from his back pocket. 'Money, I guess?' He opened his wallet to show it was empty. 'As if I've got any to hand around.'

'I don't know what I'm asking for. Nothing, I guess. It's just,' Adrian said, 'have you heard from Mum lately?'

'No.' Tom crossed his arms over his chest and snarled a

little. I didn't like the way he looked at Adrian, as though he may hit him at any moment. I was starting to think seeing Tom wasn't the best idea.

'Tom doesn't like to talk about her.' Harriet took Tom by the arm and started to nudge him towards the car. 'Come on,' Harriet said over her shoulder. 'You can at least come back to our place for a cold drink, 'ey?'

'Come on, Tom,' I heard her saying quietly as we followed along behind. 'He's your brother. We can at least offer them a bit of hospitality.'

I opened the car door and brushed numerous McDonald's wrappers onto the floor. Mum had warned me about getting into cars with strangers, but I didn't need her voice in my head to tell me this wasn't a good idea. I didn't know Harriet at all. She seemed nice, but Mum said you can't always tell when someone has had a bit to drink, or if they have taken drugs. I hesitated with one foot in the car and one on the ground.

'What's the matter?' Adrian asked from inside the car.

'Um. I, um—' I took my foot out of the car and bent down to see Adrian's face. 'Can I talk to you? Outside the car?' Tom groaned in the front passenger seat.

Adrian got out of the car and came around to my side. 'What is it?'

'We don't know Harriet,' I said. 'I don't think we should be getting into a car with someone we don't know.'

'We don't have a lot of options right now.' Frustration laced Adrian's voice.

'Maybe we should ring your mum again? See if we can get hold of her? There is no point going to Chinderah if she's not there.'

'But we have no way of getting back to Fairview either. If we go back now, we'll have no choice but to ring your parents, or Uncle Steve and Aunty Vicki, and ask them to pick us up.' The irritation in Adrian's voice was unlike him. 'How do you think it's going to go down with them?'

Mum wouldn't want me to get into a car with a stranger—she'd rather I ring her. I knew that. But if I did, this trip would be over and Adrian's mum would still be in danger. I swallowed and fought back my tears, breathing deeply. 'I don't like this,' I said.

'Neither do I. But I'm sure they don't live far from here. Goodna's not that big. It will only be a short trip and then we can work out what we're going to do from there. Come on, it will be okay.' Adrian's eyes were pleading with me. It wasn't even the cute-puppy pleading. It was the overwhelming, hopeless kind of pleading that there was no way anyone could refuse.

'Everything okay now, kids?' Tom asked as we climbed into the backseats. 'With your permission, can we drive you the three blocks to our place? Or do you need to call your mummy first, Kaitlyn?'

'It's Kathleen,' I said, heat rising to my face. 'And we would be grateful to go to your place.'

I saw Tom roll his eyes at Harriet, before she shook her head and frowned at him. I closed my eyes and prayed. If we were at Tom and Harriet's place when I opened my eyes, I would count it as a miracle.

We pulled up out the front of a brown house surrounded by shrubs. A pit bull terrier was pacing up and down a wire fence that didn't look high enough to keep him in the yard. There was a car without any number plates in the front yard and on a closer look I noticed it also didn't have any tyres.

'You live here?' I asked Harriet as we walked towards the house together. Tom and Adrian had gone on ahead of us.

'Only on the weekends,' Harriet said. 'I live on the Gold Coast. That's where I go to uni and I work as a barmaid on weeknights. I don't get much work on the weekends, so I usually come up here to see Tom. He and his housemate get pretty feral if I leave it too long before coming to see them.'

'Are you and Tom, like, together?'

Harriet laughed. 'Yes and no. We have an arrangement.'

I had no idea what that meant. I wasn't sure I wanted to know.

'What about you and Adrian?'

I shook my head. 'Not really. We kissed once, that's all.'

'You know, you don't have to kiss someone to be in love with them.' 'Is that what you meant by having an arrangement with Tom?'

Harriet squinted. 'Sort of. I love Tom, but he's in a bad place right now. I've told him I'm not committing to him until he gets his life together.'

'What do you mean, he's in a bad place?'

'He has some bad habits,' Harriet said. 'And he needs to go to TAFE, or get a job, or something proactive.' She shook her head and laughed a little. 'He's one mixed up kid. Between losing his dad and his mum going nuts, and then the stuff that prick Michael did to him...well, he's got a lot to sort through.' Harriet paused at the bottom of the steps that would take us into the house. 'Me hanging around all the time looking after him probably isn't helping much. But I'm scared about what will happen to him if I don't. Adrian was lucky to have that man take him in.'

'You mean Mr Dean? The one he lives with now?'

'Probably. Tom's never told me his name.'

A loud bang from inside the house sent Harriet and I scrambling through the front door. In the lounge room we found Adrian and Tom in a full-on brawl. Adrian was yelling something about their mum and Tom was letting loose a whole lot of words that I'd not heard before, and I was sure I was never meant to. I could see the fire in Adrian's eyes. I started yelling too, telling them to stop fighting. But Harriet stepped in between the two boys and stared Tom right in the face.

'Stop it. Now.' Her voice held authority. The two boys went quiet. 'This is not helping anyone.' She was so gentle the way she put her hand on Tom's upper arm, her eyes fixated on his face. 'Adrian,' she said, still looking at Tom, 'I imagine you are keen for Tom to care about his mum. But you have to understand that things have been different for him growing up. You can't expect him to see your mum the same way you do. It's not going to happen. He's not going to want to help her.'

Adrian frowned. 'I don't get it.'

Harriet stepped away from Tom and looked at me. 'I'll help you two out.' Tom started to complain, but she put her hand up to him. 'You don't need to be a part of this,' she said to Tom. 'This is my decision. You can't help your brother, but I can.' She turned to Adrian. 'If you can get hold of your mum, I'll drive you to the New South Wales border and meet Barbie there.' Tom went to interrupt again, but she took no notice. 'Then I'll head back to my place on the Gold Coast. I've got an assignment due Monday and my boss said he might have a shift for me tomorrow night, so I wasn't gonna hang around here for too long anyway.'

Tom shrugged. 'Whatever.'

'I'm sure you'll thank me one day.' Harriet smiled, but Tom ignored her. I really couldn't see what she saw in him.

Although I was happy to have a plan to get Adrian to his mum, my heart sank as I realised we were going to be getting into the car with Harriet again, this time for a much longer trip. Driving three blocks with her didn't make her any less of a stranger. But her confidence and ability to hold herself against the boys was impressive. I had a growing sense of respect for the woman, and the way she cared for Adrian's older brother.

I had this overwhelming feeling of having little choice in the situation. Even if I didn't know Harriet, there still weren't a lot of options at this stage—call Dad and get him to meet me in the city, or go with Harriet. My shoulder muscles ached. I longed to be back home, watching a movie with Rebecca and George on the couch, with Mum making buttered popcorn, and Dad cracking stupid jokes to make us all groan.

Tom barely acknowledged Adrian when he said goodbye, and turned on his Xbox before we'd even left the house. To make matters worse, Adrian sat in the front seat, leaving me in the back on my own. I hugged my knees to my chest. I'd never felt so far away from home.

CHAPTER 25

I wound down my window to try and get some fresh air, focusing on the trees that had pretty purple flowers, and how they carpeted the road with their colour each time the wind blew.

Harriet's little Mazda made a funny noise as we drove out towards the highway. I prayed the car would break down before we got too far, but then I thought of Adrian. If this plan didn't work, well, I wasn't sure that he could take another disappointment.

Guilt swirled around my mind, weaving through my thoughts like the Brisbane River. This was my entire fault. If only I hadn't been so caught up with Mrs Harrison being on the train, then I might not have lost my stupid purse. It was because of me that Adrian wasn't on a bus to Chinderah, that he'd had to ring his brother, and that he now had me in tow to meet his mother.

We were almost at the Ipswich motorway onramp, when Harriet pulled the car over into a KFC carpark and turned the engine off. I sighed in relief. Perhaps she had changed her mind.

'You hungry?' Adrian asked. Harriet shook her head, as my stomach rumbled. KFC always smelled so good, even if I couldn't eat it. 'Good, 'cause even if we had enough money to eat here, I don't think there's much on the menu Kat could eat.'

'No, I don't eat meat. We're not here for the food,' Harriet said.

'I said I'd only drive you if your mum can meet us at the border. I'll go as far as the New South Wales border but that's it. Call her.'

I handed Adrian my phone. 'Do you think she'll answer it, if she doesn't recognise the number?' And would Harriet still drive us, if she didn't?

'Dunno. We'll give it a try, 'ey?'

He punched in some numbers and waited, tapping his fingers along the side of the car door, just under the window. 'It rang out,' he said. He pushed more numbers and held it to his ear, his fingers strumming on the door of the car.

'Mum,' he said, turning his face towards his open window. 'Mum, it's me. Adrian.'

'Aidy!' I heard a yell through the speaker as Adrian moved the phone away from his ear for a moment.

'Yeah, yeah, Mum. I'm fine, I'm fine. How are you? Everything okay?'

Adrian nodded. He turned and smiled at me.

'Yeah, okay, Mum. Look, just hang on a sec, okay? Look, Mum, I need your help.' I could hear him sucking in breath. 'Okay, so, look, me and a friend are comin' to see you, but we've got stuck. She's lost her purse and—'

He put his hand over the phone and mumbled what sounded a lot like a swear word.

'No, Mum, not a girlfriend. Just a friend.'

A knife stabbed my heart. Harriet looked at me and smiled a half-smile. She tilted her head as if to say, 'that's tough'. I raised my eyebrows to suggest I didn't care.

'We're pretty close. We've met a friend of Tom's and she's gonna drive us to the border. Can you meet us there?' A warm breeze rustled the shrubs separating us from the highway onramp. Adrian was breathing so slightly I could barely see his chest moving. 'No, Mum, Tom's not with us.' He rolled his eyes at me and mouthed, 'Sorry.'

He continued talking to his mum. 'Yes, I've seen him, just briefly. Mum. Mum—stop please. We can talk about Tom later. Can you pick us up?' Car motors hummed along the hidden freeway. 'Mum, please. Just listen to me for a minute. I need you to come and pick me up at the border.' I could hear her muffled voice getting louder. Adrian covered the mouth piece of the phone. 'She says it's not that much further to Chinderah.'

Harriet swore. 'Tell her no!'

'Mum, it's gotta be the border. Tom's friend is already driving us all the way from Brisbane.'

I looked out the car window; white clouds dotted the otherwise perfectly blue sky. What kind of mother would refuse to come and meet her son, whom she hadn't seen for months? My mother would tell me not to judge—that I didn't know the whole story—but really, who was this woman?

'Mum, come on. If it's not that much between the border and Chinderah, why can't you drive up and meet us?' I could hear her yelling down the phone, mumbled words that didn't sound at all like yes.

'Here, give the phone to me,' Harriet said. She got out of the car and walked over to a banana tree that was offering practically no shade. I watched her throwing her spare hand up in the air and waving it around.

'What do you suppose she's saying to her?' I asked Adrian.

'No idea. But Mum was in a weird mood. If I didn't know she'd stopped drinking months ago, I'd have said she was drunk.'

I rubbed my eyes with my hands so Adrian couldn't see any fear that may have escaped onto my all-revealing face. Drunk, and yet we were hoping to get into her car—my parents would go nuts at the thought. I looked at Harriet standing at the back of the car, her hands flying around as she had an animated conversation with Adrian's mum. I marveled at her doing this for us. I reckon most people would have walked away from Tom and his family ages ago.

My watch told me it was just past four o'clock and I'd hardly eaten anything all day. I pulled a packet of lollies out of my bag and started eating them. Despite them being gluten free, they tasted so good that I'd nearly eaten the whole packet before I realised I should offer one to Adrian, and probably to Harriet as well. Harriet opened the car door, climbed into the driver's seat and slammed the door shut. 'Looks like we're goin' to Chinderah.'

Adrian mumbled an apology and said thanks.

I put my bag up against the car door and tried to get comfortable. The less I was awake, the less I knew what was going on, and the faster time would go by. And I was really starting to feel like I already knew more than what I wanted to know about Adrian's family.

We pulled off the motorway into Chinderah as the sun was painting the sky with a dusky pink colour. Adrian was asleep in the front seat and Harriet, with earphones in, was singing softly a song I didn't recognise. Her voice was sweet and I wondered again what she was doing with someone like Tom.

My stomach started voicing its opinion about the lack of decent food I'd had all day. My neck joined in on the complaining, cracking as I tried to relieve the discomfort of having slept in an unusual position. I pulled my phone out of my pocket and my heart skipped a beat. There was a missed call from my parents.

'Barbie said she'd meet us around here somewhere,' Harriet said, looking at me through the rearview mirror. She'd removed her earphones. 'I said I didn't want to know where she lives. The less I know about her, the less Tom can hate me. You two have slept most of the way. Must have been a big day for you, 'ey?'

'Yeah, you could say that,' I said, watching the way the sunset was reflecting onto the river, colouring it in its pinks and golds. This would be a lovely spot to visit under better circumstances. 'So many times today I thought we'd never get this far. Thanks so much for driving us.'

'That's okay. I've always wanted to catch a glimpse of the infamous Barbie. Figured I'd never get to meet her. Now's my chance.'

'I'm sorry we don't really have any money to offer you for petrol. I think Adrian has a bit left, but he's saving it to give to his mum in hope she'll drive us back to Fairview.'

'That's your plan?' Harriet scoffed. 'Right, good luck with that one.' My heart skipped a beat again and a knot formed in my stomach. What would we do if Adrian's mum wouldn't drive us back to Fairview?

I remembered the missed call on my mobile. I needed to call them back. Not answering the phone when either Mum or Dad called was right at the top of 'Mum and Dad's Ten Commandments': *Thou shalt not ignore a ringing phone when Mum or Dad appears on the screen.* Adrian woke just as we were pulling into a carpark with a jetty wading out into the river. There was a small white hatchback already parked not far away. A tall, thin woman with dark flowing hair stepped out of the car. I recognised her from Adrian's drawings.

Adrian opened the car door and walked towards his mum. I had expected him to run or cry, or jump up and down and fall into her arms when he saw her. But he seemed cold, almost disinterested. They hardly even hugged.

I followed behind him and when I thought they had finished saying hello, I stepped forward to stand beside Adrian. 'Hi, I'm Kat.' I extended my hand to shake Barbie's hand.

She smiled. 'Hi yourself.' Her hands were warm and soft, but bony. 'Call me Barbie.'

Harriet walked up behind us and I turned to introduce her. She was looking at Adrian's mother with a mix of sorrow and pity. 'This is Harriet. She helped us out heaps today.'

Barbie nodded.

Harriet glared at Barbie. 'I did it for Tom.' She looked at me and smiled. 'I need to get home. I've a big day tomorrow. Nice to meet you. You too, Adrian. Take care.'

'Wait, let me walk you to your car,' Barbie said and took off after Harriet.

'Mum'll be desperate for news of Tom,' Adrian said. We watched the two women talking. Barbie was being overly animated.

'She'll be lucky if she gets much out of Harriet,' I said. 'She didn't seem too impressed with your mum.' Harriet threw her hands in the air and got into her car. Barbie banged on the driver's door, but Harriet drove off.

'Certainly looking that way,' Adrian said.

As I watched Harriet drive away I couldn't help but feel a little desperate for her return. She was heading back towards Queensland and I suddenly wanted to be in the car beside her. I wanted to go back home. I wanted it so much I could hardly breathe. Adrian's mum walked back towards us and I cringed. She was little more than a walking stick. The light blue dress she was wearing hung off her, accentuating her tiny waist and lack of hips.

'She wouldn't tell me anything about Tom.' Barbie stormed back over to us. 'Useless piece of shi—'

'Mum, that's enough!' Adrian stood between his mum and me. 'She was very good to us, and to drive us all the way to here, especially. You should have been a lot nicer to her.'

Barbie glared at Adrian for a moment. 'Yeah, well, maybe. But still, she could have at least given me Tom's phone number.' She sighed. 'Come on. No use hangin' round this dump all day. Let's get goin'.'

'Wait,' I said. 'Before we do, sorry, but I need to call my parents.' I looked at Adrian. 'They tried to ring while I was asleep in the car.'

Adrian nodded.

I walked over to a seat by the river. Dad answered when I rang. I wiped my sweaty palm down my jeans. 'Dad.' I forced myself to sound as chirpy as I could manage. 'Sorry, I only just saw the missed call. What's up?'

'Oh, hi, love,' Dad said. 'I was just ringing to see if you know where Adrian ended up after you guys went shopping this morning. Mr Dean called. He's really worried because Adrian hasn't been home all day and he isn't answering his phone.'

'Oh? Adrian doesn't have any credit, so he wouldn't be able to call him back. He's probably just got his phone on silent or something.'

'Probably,' Dad said. 'But Mr Dean is really concerned. Like, really concerned, Kat. Do you know why?'

'Adrian has told me some stuff that's going on with his family, if that's what you mean.'

'What has he told you?'

'That his mum's ex-partner might be getting out of jail soon. Is that why Mr Dean is worried?'

'Yeah, that's right. We guessed Adrian would have eventually told you why he is staying with the Deans. We didn't want you to be worried about him, but it's good that you know.'

'So, has the guy got out of jail now?'

'Yes. Mr Dean is really angry that they didn't let him know sooner. He's pretty keen to talk to Adrian to make sure he is okay.'

'Well, he was with us for most of the day. I'm sure he will be home soon enough. Mr Dean shouldn't worry about him. Adrian knows what he's doing.'

'Hmm, maybe,' Dad said. 'But I also think that is why Mr

Dean is so worried. Adrian is a bit too confident about his own safety and more concerned with his mum's, when it should be the other way around.'

'Okay, well, if I hear from him, I'll be sure to tell him to get in contact with Mr Dean as soon as possible.'

'Okay, Kat. Thanks. Have you and Megan decided what you're doing tonight?'

'Yeah, I'll stay here if that's okay. I'll see you tomorrow afternoon.'

'You won't be at church?'

'It'll be easier if I just go with Megan's family to theirs. Is that okay?'

'I guess so, but I don't want you making a habit out of it. It's important that we go to church together as a family.'

'Sure, Dad. I know that. Tomorrow will be the exception. Thanks for being okay with it.'

'Well, have a good night. Don't you and Megan stay up all night chatting.'

'We won't, Dad. Love you. Night.' I closed my eyes as I hung up the phone and breathed out slowly. I hated lying. I hated having Mr Dean worrying about Adrian. I hated being so far from home and feeling hopeless and scared and not sure what to do next.

'Are we right to go, Miss Kathleen Maree?' Adrian asked as he walked up behind me. I stood up and wrapped my arms around him. 'Is everything okay?' he asked.

'Yes, and no,' I said. 'I hate lying to my family. And Mr Dean is really worried about you. He thinks you might be in danger and he's trying to find you.' I pulled out of the embrace and looked up at Adrian. 'I think you should ring him or text him or something. Maybe say you're staying over at a friend's house or something?'

'You're the only friend I've got, Kat,' Adrian said. He took my hands. 'If I text him, or ring him, he'll know it's your phone.

He'll know I'm with you and that you're not at Megan's.'

'Perhaps we could find a pay phone then?'

'Okay, we'll look out for one. Come on. Mum's getting impatient.'

I put my phone in my back pocket and walked to the car, my hand firmly placed in Adrian's. With him, I could be strong. We could get through this together. I looked at Barbie and doubted she was going to be willing to drive us back to Fairview.

I climbed into the back of Barbie's car and looked around. There were paper cups stained brown all over the floor, and enough sand to make a decent mound with my feet. The car stunk of smoke and something else—it took me a moment to recognise the smell. The same smell that was in that pink drink bottle that day at school. Alcohol. The car smelled like chocolate milk with alcohol in it.

My heart raced and I closed my eyes again. Surely she wouldn't have come to get us if she had been drinking. I wished she'd kissed me hello, then I might have smelled the alcohol on her breath. Adrian didn't look worried. I didn't know what else to do but to pray, and hope like mad that I would get to see my parents so I could tell them how very sorry I was. *Again.*

CHAPTER 26

We drove down Barbie's street with my stomach singing an unfavourable tune. I would have given anything for a dim sim smothered in soy sauce with steam rising out of a brown paper bag. The thought of eating anything, despite the gluten content, was appealing. I'd had about enough of consequences. Consequences sucked. I was sick to death of thinking about them, worrying about them, and trying to predict them.

It was quiet here, with trees lining the suburban street and not even a dog out roaming. The sun was already beginning to wrap up the day.

'Gee, I'm hungry,' I said to no one in particular. No one responded, but Adrian turned and gave me a weak smile.

I looked out the window and allowed sorrow to blanket my heart. I had, in just twelve hours, unintentionally mapped out a future for myself that I had only just begun to consider. For one thing, there was no way Mum and Dad were going to let me go to St Andrew's now. Plus, there'd be the kids at school who would hear about Adrian and I running away together and assume the worst—whatever 'worst' they could come up with in their small brains. Going back to school was going to be even more horrendous this term than it was after Megan left. I could only imagine what Paige would say about me.

A sigh escaped my lungs and rolled out of my mouth. I had failed to make the good choices Mum and Dad had wanted me to make. I had failed to show them I could make friends that wouldn't lead me astray. And perhaps the worst of all, was that I had lied to my parents again. This was it. Mum and Dad would never trust me again.

And yet, somewhere in the depth of my frustration and fear and disappointment and sadness, I knew going with Adrian had been the right decision. How could I have lived with myself, knowing he was taking this trip on his own, with practically no idea what he was doing?

Adrian's mum pulled the car over in front of a fish-and-chip shop. 'Here we are,' she said. 'Home sweet home.'

The 'S' in the shop's sign didn't light up anymore, so it read 'Fish hop'. The building, if you could call it that, was double-storey. The first floor, where the shop was, had baby-poo brown brick. Aluminium tables and chairs crowded the footpath out the front, and advertisements covered the windows. The top half of the building was weatherboard, which were crooked in places and paint was chipping off everywhere. The whole building looked tiny compared to the large lot it was on. Surrounded by dry grass that came half way up to my knee, I wondered if it was a fire hazard. I shuddered. This was where Adrian would be living if he moved back in with his mum?

'You live in a takeaway store?' I asked.

'No, not quite. I live up there.' She pointed to the rooms above the shop. An outside staircase lead to a small door with a tiny landing platform. I wondered how many people had died from standing on the platform, having knocked on the door only to be thrown off the landing when it was opened. 'But I work down here.' She smiled as though having a place and job were great accomplishments I should congratulate her on.

'That's awesome, Mum. I was so glad to hear you'd got a job and a place of your own.'

I looked at Adrian, bewildered. I'd hardly call this house, and a job in a fish-and-chip shop, something to be proud of. I rubbed my arms, suddenly aware of how cool it had gotten.

'Yeah, the boss has been real good to me.' Barbie pulled a large brown handbag out of the back of her car and tossed it over her shoulder. 'All set up by Carry, of course. And then as soon as I'd got my own place and job, she dropped me like a hot sack of potatoes. I've hardly heard from her since.'

'I guess she's pretty busy,' Adrian said.

'Yeah, busy worrying about you.' Barbie rumbled around in her bag and pulled out a cigarette. She looked at Adrian, then at me, before putting the smoke back in her pocket. 'That's all she cared about, you know. Getting you somewhere safe. I was just a little project on the side that nobody cared two hoots about.'

'That's not true, Mum. You know I care.'

Barbie shrugged and pointed to the shop. 'Are yas hungry? Shall I get some chips for dinner?'

I nodded like crazy. Adrian started questioning his mum about whether or not she could afford to buy dinner for us. His mum brushed him off and went into the shop, while Adrian and I took a seat on one of the benches out the front.

Adrian took my hand and held it in his.

'I can't believe it,' Adrian said. 'We made it.'

'Tell me about it. And your mum seems happy enough, though I don't know how she could stand to live here.'

'It's okay, and it might look better inside than it does out.' Adrian looked up at the building. 'It's going to be hard to convince her to leave here, I reckon.'

'What is your plan? What are we going to do now we're here?'

'I dunno,' Adrian said, fiddling with my fingers. 'I never got any further than this in my plans. And I didn't expect to have you with me.'

'Are you saying you wish I hadn't come along?'

'Are you kidding me? I never would have made it this far without you. I'm eternally grateful, Miss Kathleen Maree Morrow.'

'But?' I added.

'Well, I guess I'm not sure what to do, in that, I had thought that if Mum refused to come with me, that I'd just stay here. But—'

'But then how do I get home if you stay here?'

'Exactly.'

'I've been stressing ever since we left Brisbane about how we'll get back if your mum won't drive us.' Tears welled in my eyes. 'I've been wondering how we'll get back to Fairview together—I'd never thought about you staying here. I don't want to go back to Fairview without you.'

'I'm not keen to leave my mum here alone, Kat,' Adrian said. 'I can't have come all this way to just turn around and go home again. You know that.'

'I know, but I just don't understand why she isn't scared of Michael like you say she should be.'

'I remember once, back when he was living with us, Tom told her she should kick him out. Michael was being horrible to us all and Tom and I were sick of it. But she went off at Tom, saying how she was in love with Michael and that Tom should leave if he didn't like him. I guess she thought he treated her alright. But he hated Tom. And me.'

Fear shot through my heart. Mr Dean had told Dad it was Adrian everyone was concerned about with Michael's release from jail. Not his mum, not Tom, just Adrian. Why was that?

'Adrian, I don't like it here. We should just get back to Fairview and let Mr Dean sort things out with your mum. If she won't drive us, we should ask her if she could lend us some money. I'm sure my parents will pay her back for me.'

Adrian shrugged. 'I'll see if she'll come back with us, even just for a week or something. Just until I know she'll be safe and Michael isn't going to hurt her.'

The sooner we got out of this place, the better. I put my hand on my phone. Maybe I should call Dad again—he could be here by midnight if he started driving now. 'Let's go ask her,' I said.

'Ask me what?' Barbie walked out of the shop with a ticket stub in her hand.

Adrian hung his head. 'Nothing, Mum.'

'Come on, tell me. Yous 'ave come all this way. Might as well start speakin' up as to why you've come here the way you did, unexpected and all.'

I sat back down and shifted uncomfortably on the cold bench. It reminded me of the bench out the front of Mr Dean's office that had started this whole chain of events.

I looked at Adrian and cleared my throat. 'Mrs Jacobs, Adrian is keen for you to come back with us to Fairview for a while. We'd like it if you could drive us back and stay on for a while with him there.'

She made a strange snuffling sound with her breath. 'Please, call me Barbie, none of this Mrs Jacobs stuff.' She looked at Adrian. 'You've come all this way to convince me to go to Steve's place with you, have you?' Adrian shot me a look, his eyes angry, his mouth sad. I widened my eyes at him. One of us had to start talking to his mum.

Adrian breathed heavily. 'Mum, I spoke to Carry.'

'So what?' Barbie folded her arms across her chest and frowned.

'She said Michael was up for parole a few weeks back, then I spoke to her the other night and she said he was due for release any day. In fact, I reckon he's probably out already.'

'Dad told me he is,' I said. 'Just before when I spoke to him. Mr Dean had told him.'

Adrian looked at his mum.

'Really?' Barbie's face turned two shades lighter and her hands began fidgeting. 'And what's that got to do with anything?'

'I'm worried about you, Mum.'

Barbie made the scoffing sound with her breath again. She was shaking her head. 'What would he come back 'ere for? After what we did to him, dobbing him in like that and not telling 'em you was lying like he told me to say. Besides, I can take care of myself.'

'But Mum—' Adrian protested.

'What? Did you think you needed to come racing back here to protect me? Did you think Michael'd be on to me and you'd come in and save the day?' She laughed. 'And what, your girlfriend came along to help?' She wrapped her arms around her stomach and laughed so hard, she snorted.

Adrian stood up, his chair scraping on the cement and crashing to the ground as he walked off. He looked over his shoulder at me. 'You coming?'

I looked at Barbie, her eyes watering, her open mouth displaying crooked, lower teeth and the hole from what must have been a lip stud at some time. I followed Adrian. 'Where are we going?' He didn't stop.

I ran to catch up to him and grabbed his arm. 'Hey,' I said.

He stopped walking and looked at my hand on his arm. He ripped his arm from my hand. 'I'm not staying. We're going home.'

'What? Back to Fairview? How? What about your mum?'

'I don't care,' he said. 'I thought she'd changed, getting a job and all. But you saw the way she reacted when I talked about Michael. She's still in love with him. She hasn't changed.'

'Adrian.' I held both his hands in mine. 'You came here, all this way. I'm not going to let you give up just because your mother laughed at us. We can't get home anyway. We don't have enough money. The only way to get home would be to call my parents or Mr Dean, and even then, it would take them hours to get here.'

'She laughed at me. Like I'm a little kid. That's how she sees me and always will—as just a little kid.'

'That's not true. Come on, we need to go and talk to her. You need to convince her to come back with us to Fairview. We don't have a lot of choice but to go back there. We'll have something to eat with your mum and convince her that she needs to take a holiday in Fairview until we know she is safe.'

Adrian raised my hands to his lips and kept them there. I moved my head in and rested it on our entwined fingers. 'I'm so glad I'm here, Adrian. This is exactly where I should be. Here with you. It's stupid, it's crazy, it's dangerous and it's by far the worst thing I've ever done. But I still think we did the right thing to come here. You need to be here for your mum. If we leave now, you'll regret it forever.'

I felt Adrian nodding his head as my head moved up and down with his. We both giggled. He looked up and met my eyes. Then he leaned over and kissed me for the second time.

I swallowed hard. When I opened my eyes, his red eyes were looking less sad and he was smiling at me. 'You're a darn good kisser, Miss Kathleen Maree.'

'You too, Fred,' I said. 'Although, that was only the second time a boy has ever kissed me, so you know, not a lot to compare you to.'

Adrian laughed.

I looked across at Barbie, still sitting on the bench out the front of the fish-and-chip shop. She had her head down and had what looked like a large packet of chips on her lap. 'Come on. Looks like dinner is ready.' As we walked back to the shop, Adrian took my hand and squeezed it.

CHAPTER 27

While heading up the steps of Barbie's house, my muscles began to relax a little. Adrian would talk to Barbie and either she would drive us back to Fairview, or she would lend us the money so we could get back. Surely she would feel obliged to do one of those two things—Adrian was her son, after all.

Entering Barbie's house, I was confronted by the smell of something like stale bread; it left a taste of dust in my mouth. I wanted to go and open every window. Adrian didn't seem bothered by the smell, or by the clothes and takeaway containers that littered every bench and table space. She must have run out of dishes, as there were so many piled in the sink. I gasped as I noticed a trail of large black ants covering two paper plates on the bench. How could anyone live like this—let alone someone's mother?

'Mum,' Adrian said. 'What's with the kitchen? You need to clean up in here. You'll have bug issues if you keep the place like this.'

Too late, I wanted to say.

'Oh geez, get off my case, will ya?' Barbie began cleaning a place for us to sit on the couch. 'Come'n have some chips. One of you grab the dead 'orse from the fridge on your way past, 'ey?'

I looked at Adrian horrified. 'It's okay,' he said. 'She just means the tomato sauce.'

I sat on the couch next to Adrian and looked at the mass of food before us: battered fish, a couple of crab sticks, a few fried dim sims and chips covered in chicken salt. I looked at Adrian out of the corner of my eye, trying to hold back tears. Neither of us had thought to tell his mum I was gluten intolerant. There was nothing there I could eat without it causing me pain—*lots* of pain.

My stomach churned with hunger pangs. I picked up a dim sim and closed my eyes before taking a bite so big that it was more than half the fried piece of food. It was hot and chewy and salty and completely delicious. I allowed it to touch every taste bud in my mouth before swallowing and popping the rest into my mouth. I wondered how long I had before the pain would begin.

I picked up a chip and tried to brush the chicken salt off. Chicken salt doesn't have too much gluten in it. It was too late anyway—that dim sim would come back to haunt me soon enough. I knew from experience that the more gluten I ate, the worse the pain later would be. I swallowed hard. I couldn't bring myself to eat anything else.

I was so hungry my stomach was aching. I pretended to be cooling down a hot chip, but then Adrian noticed how little I was eating. 'Come on, dig in,' Adrian said before filling his mouth with a handful of chips that were too hot. He waved his hand in front of his mouth as if that was magically going to make them cool down somehow.

I blew on my chip again and smiled. I wiped as much chicken salt off as I could before popping it in my mouth.

'Come on, darl, you'll waste away at this rate,' Barbie said, throwing another dim sim in my direction. 'Have another dim sim. You ate the first one like you hadn't eaten in a week.'

I took it and rolled it between my fingers. I wanted it so bad. My stomach rumbled.

'Kat!' Adrian said, just as I was about to take a bite. 'You can't eat that.' I looked at him, my mouth open, the dim sim only centimetres from my face. 'I'm so sorry, Kat,' he said, taking it from my hand. Adrian turned to his mum, 'I forgot to mention Kat is gluten intolerant. She can't eat most of this.' He looked at me. 'Does chicken salt have gluten in it, too?'

I nodded.

'Mum, Kat can't eat any of this. I'll need to take her down and order something else.'

Barbie just shrugged and nodded. She pulled a ten dollar note out of her pocket and handed it to Adrian. 'Tell 'em you're my kid so they give us the discount.' She crossed one bony leg over the other and began thumbing something on her phone.

Adrian grabbed my hand and led me outside. 'I'm so sorry,' he said on the way down the stairs. 'I completely forgot about you being gluten intolerant for a moment. Are you okay? Did you eat much?'

I shrugged.

'Probably I should apologise about my mum, too. She's not exactly the best company. I should have warned you more about what she'd be like.'

I shook my head. 'No, it's fine,' I said. 'Did you live like that when you lived with her?'

'Yep.' Adrian sighed. 'She never was a great housekeeper. I think Dad used to do a lot of the cooking. Dad and Mum couldn't have been much more opposite. I guess that's why Mum fell apart so bad after he died. Tom said Mum used to make more of an effort, until Michael started hanging around.'

We walked into the shop and ordered the minimum chips without chicken salt and a small kabab without the bread wrap. The guy with the white apron and bushy beard behind the counter wrote down the order. 'Ten minutes give or take,' he said.

'I might just ring Dad,' I said to Adrian. 'See what's happening, you know, with Mr Dean being worried about you and all.'

'Don't tell them where I am, though, will you?' Adrian said.

I smiled and nodded the promise.

Outside the shop, I dialled Dad's mobile number and began walking towards the street corner. There was a phone box at the end of the street and I turned to tell Adrian, thinking he could ring his uncle, but he'd disappeared from view.

'Hey, Kathleen,' Dad said. 'Is everything okay?'

'Fine, Dad, thanks. Just wondering if Adrian got home alright?'

'Adrian home?' Dad said. 'No. Mr Dean has called the police and they're out looking for him. Why? Have you heard from him? If you know anything, you need to tell us.'

The phone went slippery in my hand. What was I supposed to say?

'Um, well,' I said. 'I shouldn't be telling you this, but he was talking about going to see his mum. He thought she might have been in some sort of trouble.'

'Kathleen,' Dad said. 'This is serious. I mean really serious. Is Adrian there with you now?'

'No,' I said, which was technically true. I wasn't exactly sure where he had gone.

'Are you sure?' Dad asked.

I heard a car horn in the background of Dad's phone. 'Dad, are you going somewhere? Are you in the car?'

Dad paused. I could hear him breathing down the phone. 'Yes. I'm actually with Mr Dean. We're out looking for Adrian.'

'Oh.'

'This is very serious. If you know something, please, tell us.'

'Okay.' I swallowed hard. How to obey my dad, yet keep my promise to Adrian. 'I can't tell you anything, Dad, other than that Adrian is safe.'

I could hear Dad whispering something, and what sounded like Mr Dean responding.

'Kathleen,' Dad said. 'I need you to listen to me. You're both in danger. We know you're not at Megan's. Do you know exactly where Adrian is?'

'Sort of. I can't see him at the moment. We're getting fish and chips for dinner. Barbie got us some, but we forgot to say about me being—'

Dad interrupted. 'You are at his mum's?'

'I, err—' I promised I wouldn't tell!

'Kathleen!'

'Okay, yes, we're at Adrian's mum's place in Chinderah. But I don't see what the problem—'

'Kathleen!' Dad yelled down the phone. 'This is very important. Listen to me. I want you to go and find Adrian and get away from the house immediately. Just walk away, anywhere but there. Use your phone to find where the nearest police station is and head in that direction. Do you understand?'

Adrian walked around the corner and waved the receipt from the fish-and-chip shop. Our order must have been ready. Dad was still yelling down the phone.

'Okay, Dad, sure. I gotta go.' I hung up the phone, even though Dad was still yelling at me. A chill flowed down my spine.

'Everything okay?' Adrian asked.

I smiled weakly and nodded. 'Are the chips ready?'

'Should be. Let's go get them.'

My phone started ringing again, so I flicked it to silent.

'Your dad?' Adrian asked.

I nodded. 'He'll be right. I'll call him again later.'

We walked into the fish-and-chip shop, my heart still racing from my conversation with Dad. If it were true, and Adrian was in danger, then he would assume his mum was too. How could I get him to walk away with me? Nothing I could think of would make him leave his mum if he thought Michael was on his way to get her.

The man behind the counter wiped his hands on the white apron hanging from his waist.

'Youse Barbie's kids?' He picked up the cage of fries and heaved them out of the deep fryer, dumping them on a sheet of white paper.

'Yes,' Adrian said. 'But just me. This is my friend.'

The man looked Adrian over. 'You don't look much like her,' he said.

'They reckon I take after my dad,' Adrian said.

'I reckon you don't look much like 'im either,' the man said, wiping his hands on his apron again before picking up the salt.

'Just plain salt, please,' I said. The man nodded and grabbed a different shaker.

'My dad?' Adrian asked.

'Yeah,' the man said. 'I hope it's just his looks they say you take after. Geez he's a piece of work. No offence, kid.'

'My dad?' Adrian asked again.

'There's been a real change in your mum since he came back, too,' the man said. 'She's been real quiet at work and not always turning up for her shifts. One night, it was a quiet Wednesday night, and she fell asleep right at the counter 'ere. She'd never done anything like that before.'

'My dad?' Adrian said again.

My heart leapt into my mouth and dread swept over my body, causing it to shudder.

'Adrian,' I whispered. 'He's talking about Michael.' That was why Dad said we were in danger. It's because Michael was already here. Already here—with Adrian's mum.

'Michael?' Adrian said. It was like his mouth was talking

but his brain had gone somewhere else.

'Yeah, that's 'im,' the man said. 'Turned up end of last week and moved in upstairs without even talkin' to me. I mean, I'm a reasonable guy, ya know. But you're supposed to let yer landlord know when someone new moves in. Anyway, he's alright, other than he's having what I'd call a negative effect on yer mum. And she's been one of me best workers here in a long while.'

I looked at Adrian. His face looked as white as mine felt. 'The white Ford that's around the back, is that his?' Adrian pointed to where he had just come from.

'Yeah, that's his. I saw 'im drive in about five minutes ago.'

'So he's upstairs?'

'I'd reckon so,' the man behind the counter said. 'He's come and gone a bit, but if his car's there, he is too.'

I shook my head. 'We have to leave, Adrian,' I said. 'We need to get out of here now.'

Adrian looked at the man before he turned and walked out of the shop. 'Adrian, wait!' I called.

'Oi, pay me first,' the man said. 'You might be Barbie's kids but that doesn't mean I trust you to pay later for your food.' I could hear Adrian thumping up the steps to his mum's front door.

I chucked the money Barbie had given us to the man. 'I think, maybe, you should ring the police?'

'What?' The man wiped his hands on his white apron again. 'You expecting trouble?'

I held the bag of food to my chest, allowing its warmth to seep into my chilled body.

'I don't know. Maybe.'

I headed after Adrian. I could hear yelling. My vision became blurry with tears; I could hardly see the steps in front of me. What had we done? We never should have come here!

There was more yelling—Barbie's voice. And definitely two

male voices. I placed the chips on one of the steps and crept to the landing. There were a couple of lights on in the kitchen. I could see Barbie, hunched over on the floor, sobbing, holding her stomach.

I made eye contact with her and started to move towards her, but the look on her face stopped me. Her eyes were filled with terror. 'Leave!' she mouthed to me. I started stepping backwards, and was almost back onto the landing, when I heard the yelling start again. My shoes became lined with gum. I managed to get one foot in the air just as Adrian's distressed voice rang out. Wood pounded on wood, then my bones chilled as the sound of skin landing on skin echoed down the hall. I needed to go to him, to see if he was okay—to do something. But I just stood there, watching.

Adrian came running out of a bedroom down the hall and straight to his mum. He was trying to pick her up. A man, tall and thin, stepped into the hallway. He had dark eyes and dirty brown skin that hung onto him like an oversized singlet. Adrian tried again to pick Barbie up, dragging her a few centimetres towards the doorway.

'I'm here for you, boy. You coward, running away to Queensland. Did you think you'd be safe up there? Do you really think you'll be safe anywhere?' He laughed, his face looking at the ceiling. 'All you did was save me the trip.' The man snarled at Adrian, but then his lips turned to a grin as he pulled out a small knife.

'No!' I yelled. The man turned and looked at me with a surprised look on his face. I heard Adrian yell. There was deep breathing, scuffling, movement, furniture, more yelling.

Adrian wrestling with the man with the knife.

Barbie lay motionless on the floor. Adrian crumbled beside her as red liquid splattered across the floor. I screamed. There was a deafening thumping coming from behind me, loud voices circled around me and then a sudden, searing pain in my left shoulder. The room began to spin. Then it went black.

CHAPTER 28

Light poured into the room from a large window to my right and a series of familiar-sounding beeps was coming from a machine beside me. I blinked a few times before looking around. A thin blanket lay over my body and when I went to sit up, pain shot down my side and arm. I looked across to see my arm was heavily bandaged all the way up to my shoulder; a tube ran out of it and up into a bag of clear liquid attached to a thin pole.

My tongue was thick and kept sticking to the roof of my mouth, while my throat was dry and sore. There was a glass of water with a straw by my bedside table, but I wasn't able to reach it. As I leaned a little to the side to see if I could get closer, my head began to throb. I relaxed back into my pillow and closed my eyes.

I scanned my memories. I thought of my last day of school term and of my birthday trip to Movie World. I remembered Dad and the anxiety attack he'd had on the way home from the Deans' house. And I thought of Megan. And Adrian.

Adrian! I pulled myself up into a seating position and waited for the room to stop spinning. Then, swinging my legs over the side of the bed, I heaved myself off and planted my feet on the white floor. I felt as though I'd just run up a flight of stairs.

Mum's voice flowed in from outside the room.

'Mum?' I called out.

Straightaway her head poked around the door. 'Kat!' She embraced me and began scolding me at the same time. 'You need to hop back into bed. Doctor's orders!' Mum swung my legs around. 'How are you feeling? Do you need anything?' I indicated to the water and she held it for me while I drank. 'Not too much,' she said. 'Just small amounts to start with or it could make you sick.'

'My throat hurts.'

Mum nodded. 'You've had surgery, so they had a tube down your throat. Do you remember why?'

I shook my head. 'I remember being at Mrs Jacobs' place. I remember lots of yelling, and Mrs Jacobs lying on the floor.' I rubbed the side of my head and found it hurt. 'Why does my head hurt?'

'You fell and hit your head on the way down. The police think it was a side table. Don't think about things too much just yet. The main thing right now is that you and Adrian are okay.'

I gasped. 'Adrian! The knife—there was a man with a knife!'

'Yes, Kat.'

'Adrian. Is he okay?'

Mum looked worried. 'You don't remember me telling you before?'

I shook my head. 'I've been asleep, haven't I?'

'Hmmm. This is the third time you've woken since coming out of theatre. The doctor says it's normal after experiencing the kind of shock you have just been through.'

'Mum, what about Adrian?'

'He is okay,' Mum said, gently patting my hair and running her hand down my face.

'But?' My hands began shaking.

'But he was injured in the attack, as well.'

'As well?' I looked again at my bandaged shoulder. 'I was stabbed? That's the pain in my shoulder?'

Mum nodded. 'Adrian's okay, but it was a much more serious injury than yours. Oh, Kathleen, we were so worried about you. About both of you. I just can't understand why you felt you needed to get involved in all of this.'

'He needed me, Mum,' I said. 'He wouldn't rest until he knew his mum was safe. And he couldn't have got to Chinderah without my help. He's a dunce when it comes to travelling on trains and all that sort of thing. I'm so sorry, Mum. I shouldn't have lied, but you never would have understood. No one understood. That's why we had to go in secret.'

'It's okay, it's okay. Don't get yourself upset,' Mum said. 'It's all okay now.'

I took some deep breaths and rested back into the pillow. 'What happened to Mrs Jacobs?'

Mum sat down by the bed and took hold of my good hand. She stroked it gently, running her fingers down the veins.

'You have good veins, you know,' she said. 'Easy to find in an emergency. Your dad said the ambulance officers were commenting on them when he met them at the hospital.'

'Dad's here?'

Mum nodded. 'He's been here the whole time. He and Mr Dean were on their way to Chinderah when the police rang and told them what happened. They were able to go straight to the hospital and meet you not long after the ambulance arrived. Dad's down in the cafe with Rebecca and George now, but they'll be back up soon. They'll be glad to see you're awake and looking so good, especially George. We've all been very worried about you.'

I smiled and shrugged. 'Nice to be loved.'

'You know,' Mum said, 'it was just as well the police arrived when they did. Who knows what would have happened if you hadn't told your dad the truth. Mr Dean wouldn't have been able to call the police and get them to go around and investigate.

They walked in just in time.'

'So, Adrian's mum?'

'She was the only one who escaped relatively unharmed, other than some bruising and a couple of cracked ribs. It seemed everyone had been right—Michael was only there in order to get to Adrian. It was Adrian he'd wanted to hurt all along.'

'That's not what Adrian believed.'

'That's because Michael convinced Adrian that he would hurt his mum if Adrian ever told anyone about Michael's abuse.'

'Then why, and how, did Michael manage to stab me?' I ran my hand up and down the roughness of my shoulder bandage.

Mum smiled. 'The police think you were just in the wrong place at the wrong time. Michael threw the knife at the police as they came in the door behind you. Turns out he was a bad throw. It was just unfortunate that he managed to throw it so it went into your shoulder.'

'Oh.'

'But, if it wasn't for you, there's a fair chance Adrian wouldn't still be with us.' Mum stood up and smoothed out the bed covers. 'Not that I'm terribly impressed by the way you put yourself in danger. But apparently you called out and distracted Michael. The police are sure that things would have ended more seriously for Adrian if you hadn't distracted Michael when you did.'

The panic attacks began that night in hospital. Sometimes I would dream of black figures moving through rooms being chased by human-sized knives, or I'd see images of Adrian lying on a piece of white paper as though he had been absorbed by one of his drawings and he was trapped, unable to get out. I'd wake up thinking my heart had stopped beating and I was falling through my bed into an abyss. I became scared to go to sleep. It was worse when the doctor gave me a sleeping tablet, too, because it was so much harder to pull myself out of the dream. A psychologist came to see me when the panic attacks started during the day as well. She was nice, and didn't make me feel like I was going insane—well, not much, anyway.

Mr Dean came to visit me while I was in hospital. I wasn't sure how happy he would be to see me, but he said he was glad that I was okay, that both Adrian and I were okay. He had brought with him a card as big as my pillow that had been signed by Mrs Anderson and most of the kids in my form class.

'School has started back already?' I asked.

Mr Dean nodded. 'Everyone was upset to hear about you and Adrian—Mrs Anderson especially. She wanted to deliver you this card herself, to make sure you really were okay.' I opened the card. Veronica wrote how amazing she thought I was and how she hoped we might be friends one day. Keira signed her name with two kisses. It looked like everyone in the class had signed it, though I couldn't see Paige's name anywhere.

As Mr Dean stood talking to Dad about Adrian and how worried he had been at the thought of losing him, I thought about what it must have been like for him. He'd been driving around trying to find Adrian, knowing he could have been in danger, and I had been trying to stop him.

As Mr Dean said goodbye, I decided I needed to put a few things right. 'Wait, please,' I said. He sat in the chair beside my bed, putting an overnight bag on the floor beside him. 'Before you go, I need you to know, to understand, how sorry I am for lying to you and my dad, Mr Dean.' I swallowed back my tears. 'I'm especially sorry for not telling you where Adrian was, when you were so worried about him. I realise now how wrong that was of me.'

Mr Dean nodded and sighed deeply. 'It's okay, Kat.' He looked at me, sincerity in his eyes. 'I forgive you. It seems Adrian was going to find Barbie with or without you, and for the most part, I'm glad he wasn't alone. I wish, of course, you'd never been hurt.

I have my own regrets, my own part to play in what happened.' Mr Dean stood up. 'I guess what I'm trying to say is, we all have things to take away and learn from this. I'm just glad everyone is going to be okay.' There was a sadness now in his eyes—the same expression he'd worn months ago when he'd tried to convince me to tell the truth while a pink drink bottle had sat in the middle of his desk. It was the kind of look that filled me with regret. There had been so many adults who had only wanted what was best for both Adrian and me—and I'd let them all down.

When Dad came back to my room, I asked him to sit beside me. 'You know how sorry I am, don't you, Dad?'

Dad nodded. 'I believe you when you say you're sorry, honey.'

I breathed in and held the air in my lungs for a moment. 'I want to move on, to not keep dwelling on what I should have done and how I could have done things better, because it is eating me up inside. But I think that before I can start doing that, there are some people I still need to apologise to.'

'Oh? Such as who?'

'Well, Mrs Harrison for a start.' I let out a sigh. 'She was on the train with us on Saturday morning. I panicked and lied to her about what we were doing there that day. I want her to know how sorry I am.'

Dad smiled. 'I'm sure you'll have the chance to tell her yourself on Sunday. She'd like to hear it from you.'

I nodded.

'You know, Mrs Harrison had called me when she got to Brisbane to say she'd seen the both of you and how odd the whole thing had been. Mr Dean was already wondering where Adrian was, and it was her phone call that made us worried. If she hadn't rung, things could have ended differently.'

'We must have looked really suspicious for her to ring you.'

'I don't know; she rang initially to let us know she found

your purse on the floor of the train. She'd tried to call out to you before you got off, but you hadn't heard her.'

'Wow.' I chuckled. 'And here I was, at that point, still thinking we'd gotten away with so much.'

'Hmm, well, it seems your mother isn't the only one who has an eye for lying.'

George burst into the room and climbed up onto the bed, snuggling in under my good arm. I laughed. 'Hi, Georgie. What's up?'

'Mum says we can go h-h-home today!' he said. George's face lit up with his accomplishment and he beamed at Mum and Rebecca as they walked into the room.

'That's great talking, George!' Rebecca and I said at the same time, sending George into a giggle fit.

***

With my bags packed and ready to go, I said a quiet goodbye to my hospital room. A sunbeam flowed through the window to rest at my feet; I knew I was walking away a different person. This was it, the fresh start I had been looking for. It was right here, within me. I had changed.

'Can I see Adrian before we go?' I asked as Mum picked up my bag.

Mum and Dad looked at each other quickly, then Dad shook his head. 'No, not yet. Sorry, honey. I know you must be keen to see him, but he's still only having family visit at the moment. The hospital has pretty strict rules when it comes to visiting patients in the ICU ward.'

'When will he get out of hospital?'

'Adrian's injuries were worse than yours,' Mum said. 'Relatively speaking, your wound was simple to fix. But Adrian's is more complicated. He'll need more surgeries over the next few weeks.'

'Oh. And then what?'

'You'll see him again, if that's what you mean,' Dad said. 'Things are very up in the air right now, but Mr Dean is keen for him to come home to Fairview.'

I nodded and smiled, but I couldn't help but feel really sad. Adrian was here, in the same building as me, injured, with hardly anyone in the world who cared about him—and I wasn't allowed to see him.

As we made our way down the hospital corridor, a girl with a bunch of coloured balloons walked past us. 'Mum, can I buy something for Adrian?' I asked.

She looked at Dad, who nodded. 'We can organise for it to be sent up to him, I'm sure.'

There was a small stationery shop that also sold books and magazines nearby. I went straight to the paper section where I found a large sketchpad. Next to it was a packet of grey lead pencils. I walked over to the magazines until I found the perfect one called *Destinations*. A variety of countries and their top tourist spots were splashed across the front. 'Perfect,' I said. 'Do you mind, Mum? It might cost a bit.'

Mum pulled out her purse. 'Not at all.'

I placed the items on the shop counter. 'Do you want this sent to a patient here in the hospital?' The lady behind the counter was kind-faced.

'If that is possible, yes please,' I said.

'Here's some small cards to choose from. I'll attach it to the gift,' she said.

I decided on a card with a single blue balloon on it. 'He's in the ICU ward. Is that going to be okay?'

The lady behind the counter nodded. 'If not, the nurse will keep it until the patient is well enough to receive it.' She had a calm, soothing voice—very appropriate for a hospital setting.

I gave the pen to Mum. 'Could you write it please? I'm not so good at writing with the sling on.'

'Sure.' Mum took the pen.

'Just write: *Remember, you don't ever have to be bored when you can escape into your mind and go exploring. Stay brave, Fred.*'

Mum laughed. 'Fred?'

'It's a long story.' I smiled, remembering that first day in detention. I knew a whole lot more about being brave now than I had back then.

'Don't you want to sign your name, so he'll know who it's from?'

I shook my head. 'He'll know.'

CHAPTER 29

I stood at the bathroom mirror, brushing my hair straight down past my shoulders. I'd never really liked my hair: not curly enough to be pretty, not straight enough to be fashionable. It was somewhere in the middle that made it difficult to do anything much with.

At least my dress looked okay. Grandma had sent some money to buy a dress for the graduation dinner. Mum and I had gone on three shopping trips, including a train ride to the Sunshine Coast, before we found the perfect dress. I adjusted the lemon waistline so the dress fell into a soft, full skirt down to my knees. I wished Adrian were going to be there tonight. I think he would have liked my dress.

'Do you want me to do your hair, Kat?' Rebecca asked from the bathroom doorway. 'I could get my curling wand if you want.'

I nodded. 'Oh, yes please. Thanks. That would be awesome.'

George ran into the bathroom and hit my legs with a thud. His big brown eyes looked up from in amongst the bottom of my dress. 'Oooo, pretty, Kathlee!' He said.

I ruffled his hair. 'You're taller, George. I'm sure you've grown.' He grinned, showing off his recently lost bottom tooth. 'But next, we've really got to work on putting the "n" at the end of my name.'

Rebecca worked on my hair for twenty minutes, getting

the curls to sit just right. As she was spraying her work with hairspray, she said, 'You need a clip to put here. It will make the curls in your fringe fall nicely. I'll see what I have in my room.' While she was gone, I found a plain gold clip in the shape of a heart in the bathroom drawer that I'd never seen before. It was just what I needed for the night. Moving my injured arm into position, I clipped my fringe into place and smiled.

'I found one!' I called out. Rebecca agreed the clip was perfect and declared me ready for graduation.

'Wow, look at you!' Mum grinned as I walked into the lounge room.

'Where did my little girl go?' Dad said, wiping a pretend tear from his cheek. I swatted him with my good arm.

'You look fabulous, Kat,' Mum said. 'Very grown up.'

'Thanks.'

George walked into the room and held up a red toy for me to see.

'Who's that?'

'I-on Man,' George said, flying the toy across my face.

I looked at Mum. 'He means Iron Man. Another Grandma toy.' Mum rolled her eyes. 'I'm trying to just let go and roll with it.'

'Where's Batman?' I asked George. He shrugged his shoulders and he, with Iron Man, exited the room in a burst of pretend firepower.

'Moving on, huh?' I said.

'Thank goodness,' Mum said. 'Though I'm hardly thrilled with the new obsession.'

I laughed.

'Speaking of moving on,' Mum said. 'Have you made a decision yet?'

'Yes,' I said, taking a deep breath. 'I'm going to stay at Central High.'

Mum and Dad looked at each other, surprised. 'You do know there's still a very good chance Adrian won't be here next year.'

'Yeah, I know. But I think going to St Andrew's with Megan is the easy option. Harder for us as a family, but easier for me. And everyone has been so nice to me at school this term, helping by taking notes for me in class, and offering to carry my books. And, well, I guess maybe the teachers care about me more than I was willing to realise.'

Dad put his arm around Mum and squeezed.

'Yeah, so, I think I'm ready for the challenge of staying. You know, I managed to put this hair clip in myself.'

'I recognise that clip,' Mum said. 'I bought it on our last train trip to Sydney, just a few months after George was born. Where ever did you find it?'

'It was just in the bathroom drawer. Sorry, Mum. Here, I'll take it out.'

'No, no,' Mum said. 'It's perfect.'

Mum began packing things for George into a small backpack. 'We're just about ready to go.'

Dad snuck up beside me. 'Are you sure you don't want to go to St Andrew's, Kat? Your mum and I have it sorted. We even have a laptop lined up for you to use.'

I shook my head. 'St Andrew's will always be there if I change my mind, right?'

Dad nodded and smiled. 'I'm so proud of you.'

I sighed. The mistakes I'd made and the lies I'd told had found forgiveness. Tonight's graduation dinner would mark a new stage in my life. If only Adrian was there to share the moment with me.

Dad grabbed the keys while Mum yelled out to George and Rebecca that they should be in the car already. She motioned for me to head out the door, too.

'I'll be there in a second.' I tucked my phone into my hand and headed to the bathroom. In front of the mirror, I looked myself over, happy with the picture I saw in front of me. I pulled out my phone and took a selfie. I clicked on Messages and typed in Adrian's name, adding the comment: 'Wish you were going to be there tonight. You're the only one I would have wanted to go with.' I pushed send.

The school's function room was full of people, noise, music and decorations. It had been a long time since I'd been in a crowd this big. I steadied my breathing, as my psychologist had taught me to do, and focused on it. I was determined not to have a panic attack tonight. I grabbed Dad's hand and plastered a smile on my face, glad in my decision to not accept a date to take for the dinner. I felt safe with Dad walking me in, confident that I could do this.

A large board at the door, covered in blue and mauve streamers, had the seating chart. I looked down the list to find my name. I was sitting next to Veronica and a boy from one of the other classes. I nodded, but my heart was empty. I just wanted Adrian to be here.

With thumping in my chest and a clammy hand in Dad's, I scanned the room to find the table that would have my name on it. According to the seating board, it was on the other side of the room—but there was a sea of people between me and there. What had I said about accepting new challenges? Surely this was a good place to start. I could see Mr Dean talking to students as they gathered around the room.

I smiled at Mum and Dad and shrugged. 'I guess I'd better go on my own from here.'

Mum kissed me on the cheek. 'I couldn't be prouder of you,' she said. 'Enjoy your dinner.' George reached up for a cuddle and a sloppy kiss.

Rebecca gave me a soft hug and whispered, 'Crazy, I know, but I'm pretty cool with being your sister tonight. You look awesome.'

'Don't,' I said. 'You don't want my mascara to run, do you?'

Dad pulled me into a tight embrace. 'Have a great night. You deserve to celebrate all you've achieved these past few months. We're super proud of you.' I think he wiped away a tear as he turned to head back to the car—and he wasn't pretending this time.

I weaved my way through the crowd, smiling at a few random people, trying not to make too much eye contact along the way. My knees were wobbly; I was glad I had accepted Mum's advice to stick with my silver sandals, rather than buy a pair with heels like Veronica had suggested. Veronica waved and smiled, tossing her hair over her shoulder. I waved back and quickly looked away. She looked gorgeous. Maybe it was better Adrian wasn't here—how could I ever compete with girls like Veronica around?

The room felt enormous and yet was full of people. These were the people I had spent years of my school life with, but the one person I wanted to be there, wouldn't be. I took a deep breath. A few people were already sitting at the large round table, but they were sullen and quiet. One of them was Mercy.

'Hey, Mercy,' I said. 'You look pretty. Pink suits you.'

She smiled and her cheeks burst into beetroot red, clashing with her dress. 'Ah, yeah. Thanks. You look real, um, Barbie-doll-ish.' I chuckled, not sure if that was supposed to be a compliment or not.

As I sat down, everyone was looking in my direction, but it wasn't me they were looking at. 'Hey, Kat.' I turned around to see Keira standing behind me.

'Keira! Hi! How are you?' Keira hadn't spoken to me since before the incident in Chinderah, so this was a bit weird.

'You look nice. Interesting colour choice, though—yellow.'

I ignored the insult. 'Thanks, you look nice, too,' I said, putting my new lying skills into practise. Her dress was all black, except for some dark red jewels around the neckline, and was so short that I wondered if it was supposed to be a top, not a dress. I was surprised she could stand in her heels, let alone walk, they were so high. 'I see you've dyed your hair black.'

'Have you heard?' Keira asked. I noticed that underneath her fringe, her eyes were red and puffy.

'No? What's the matter?'

'It's Paige,' Keira said. 'She's gone.'

'Gone? What do you mean?' I turned in my seat so I could face Keira. Her hands were shaking. Veronica stepped up beside her, with Jessica close behind, as usual. Veronica placed her hand on Keira's shoulder.

'They took her away,' Keira said in between sobs.

'Who did? What's going on?' I looked at Veronica, who looked genuinely sad. 'Do you know?'

Veronica leaned in closer towards me. 'Child Protection came and took her away this morning, according to Mrs Anderson. Apparently, it wasn't just cigarettes she was smoking.'

I gasped. 'They took her away?'

Keira nodded. 'Someone must have rung them.'

'I heard it was more than just what she was smoking,' Jessica said, bubbling with her news of Paige. 'There was some strange stuff going on in that house—her step-dad was one weird guy.'

I shook my head—how would Jessica know anything? I turned and focused on Keira. 'What about her mum? Why doesn't she come back and get her?'

Keira shrugged and used a napkin from the table to try and wipe away the black line of mascara that was running down her face. 'Paige's been trying to find her for weeks. No one knows where she is.' Keira turned to Veronica. 'Is it all gone?' Veronica reached into her clutch and pulled out a small mirror, holding it up so Keira could look into it.

Tears welled in my eyes; it wasn't fair! Paige didn't deserve this. 'This is awful! Isn't there someone who will take her in? Her grandma or someone?'

Veronica shook her head. 'Mrs Anderson said she'll go to a foster family when they find someone for her and her little sister. She said they still might get to stay in Fairview, if they find someone here who can take them both. But then there's the problem of her step-dad to deal with. Really, she could end up anywhere in Queensland.'

I shuddered in disbelief. 'Isn't she too old to go into foster care?'

'Apparently not,' Veronica said, her eyes rolling a little as she spoke.

'Paige will hate it,' Jessica said. 'She's too much of a free spirit for fostering. I bet she'll be on Jim Valencia and Rick Harvard's couch before long.'

'Who?' I asked.

'A couple of senior boys she's been hanging around with. They live in their own flat.' Jessica waved her hand around as though that was supposed to explain everything.

'Isn't it all just horrible?' Keira said. 'I don't know how I will get through senior school without Paige.' She burst into tears again.

Veronica put her arm around Keira. 'It's okay. You can join our group, can't she, Kat? We'll be there for you. Okay?'

Keira nodded and brightened a little. I felt sick to my stomach. Was she really only concerned about herself and how Paige's troubles would affect her? My shoulder began throbbing and I could feel pain starting to surge up from my neck muscles into the back of my head. I could feel my mind becoming cloudy.

I needed to get out, fast. 'I think I need some air.'

Veronica smiled at me. 'It's okay, Kat. We'll come get you if you're not back for when they start serving dinner. Everyone will understand.'

I didn't know if having Veronica's sympathy was comforting or nauseating. I put my fingers in my ears and worked my way through the sea of people to the side door of the room, breathing deeply as I stepped out into the fresh night air.

My whole body begin to expel the tension. I wasn't sure how I was going to manage sitting around talking chit-chat to those girls over dinner.

'Hey,' came a voice through the darkness. 'You aren't supposed to be out here.' I peered out, waiting for my eyes to adjust to the lack of light. There was an outline of a head, and a hoodie that was pulled over it.

As my eyes adjusted, I realised the person was in a wheelchair.

CHAPTER 30

I struggled to look at the face speaking to me in the darkness.

'Hey, Miss Kathleen Maree Morrow,' Adrian said, lifting his head.

I squealed—in what I would consider to be a true girly squeal—and threw my arms awkwardly around his neck. 'What are you doing here? Are you okay? Should you be here?'

He laughed. 'It's okay. I'm here as a surprise for you, actually.'

'What?' I laughed, planting a big kiss on his cheek.

His grin was excessive. 'Your parents had told Uncle Steve how disappointed you'd been that I wouldn't be here for graduation from middle school. And, you know, me too. I mean, I couldn't miss seeing you dressed up like a princess now, could I? So, he organised it with the hospital.'

I knelt beside him, holding his hand. 'So, are you okay?'

'Pretty much.' He indicated to his feet and he lifted them one at a time. 'The doc reckons just one more operation should do the trick. Then it'll be a bit more physio and I'll be as good as new.'

'As good as new, huh?' I smiled.

'Or better. How about you? How you doing?'

'Okay. About a thousand million times better now that you're here.'

'How's the shoulder?'

‘Oh look, I’ll show you my new party trick.’ I moved my arm across my body and placed my hand up on my head where Mum’s clip rested in my hair.

‘Wow, that’s cool.’

‘Sure is.’ We sat in silence for a moment. ‘How’s your mum?’

Adrian shrugged. ‘She’s okay. Aunty Vicki has been picking Mum up from rehab on Sunday afternoons so she can come in and see me. Once she finishes spending the first fifteen minutes crying and telling me how sorry she is and how she is going to make it all up to me, we’ve managed to have some decent conversations. About the future and stuff.’

‘Oh? The future?’

‘Yeah. It’s hard to think about it too much, but we both want to move forward, so we need to make sure we’re planning for that.’

I nodded and smiled without sincerity. I knew this was the most likely outcome; living with his mum was what Adrian had been hoping for. But I wanted so badly for him to stay in Fairview, even if we could only ever be friends. Not getting to see him all term, other than Skype calls to the hospital and texting, had been awful. I’d really missed him at school—missed seeing that stupid hoodie pulled up over his face, his black fringe sticking out at the front. Missed sitting in class, bored, and not being able to watch his pencil come alive as he worked his magic over a piece of paper.

Suddenly Mr Dean burst outside, his face red as he puffed. ‘Kat, you’re here. You found him.’

I nodded. ‘Sorry, Mr Dean, I didn’t mean to. I just needed some air after Keira told me about Paige.’

‘Yes, I’m sorry about that. I wanted to tell you myself, but I got caught up talking with some parents. And then, well, I was supposed to come and get Adrian once you’d arrived. Your parents and I wanted it to be a surprise for you.’

‘Well, it sure was that.’ I bent down and hugged Adrian again. ‘Best surprise ever.’

Mr Dean looked embarrassed. ‘We…argh…we need to go in now. They’ve already started serving first course and I’m supposed to be making an announcement, welcoming everyone.’

I stood behind Adrian’s wheelchair and began to push. ‘Do you mind if I wheel him in?’

‘That would be great. Thanks, Kathleen.’ Mr Dean held the door open and we went through.

As we walked towards the table I was seated at, I noticed the girls making room for Adrian. Veronica winked at me as she removed the chair that had been beside mine. There was a mumble throughout the room and it felt as though every eye in the room was watching us. But I smiled—this is exactly where I wanted to be, here with Adrian. I sat down and held Adrian’s hand tight—his was shaking even more than mine.

As we ate our meals, Mr Dean went through the schedule for the night. I knew nothing but Adrian sitting beside me. Veronica chatted to him like they were old friends and Mercy stared at him all evening. Adrian had become a legend in his absence. But it was my hand he held, and my eyes he looked into when Veronica asked a question that he didn’t want to answer.

There could have been only the two of us in the room and it would have made no difference to me. As dessert was served, a band began playing in the corner. They were four students from senior school. The lead singer was tall and lanky with hair that stuck straight up towards the ceiling. He kept yelling out, ‘Come on, sing along!’ to every song they played. It didn’t take long before people began getting up to dance, which meant I finally had Adrian all to myself.

‘You know, we could have a go at dancing,’ Adrian said.

I laughed. ‘That would be a sight.’

Adrian winked at me. 'I'm better than you think. Let's give it a go.'

I wheeled Adrain through the maze of chairs, out onto the edge of the dance floor, and helped Adrian flip up the footrests of his wheelchair. Holding firmly onto my arm, he stood up, wobbly at first, and slightly bent at the knees. He let go once he was steady and began unzipping his hoodie. His eyes sparkled as they held my gaze. He opened the hoodie to reveal a crisp white shirt and yellow tie underneath. For the first time, I saw Adrian Jacobs as he really was: bright blue eyes, strong jaw line, dimples when he smiled, ears that stuck out a little, and wavy hair as it flowed down over the back of his neck. I laughed and cried at the same time.

Someone in the room started clapping. Before long we had the attention of most of the room. It made me laugh all the more. I figured this was about as close to being famous as either Adrian or I would ever be; unless Adrian became a renowned artist, which was very possible.

'I couldn't be prouder of you,' Mr Dean said, appearing beside us. 'Of both of you, really.'

Adrian leaned over and hugged his uncle.

'Have you let her in on our little secret yet?' Mr Dean asked, as he helped Adrian sit back down in the wheelchair.

Adrian smiled and shook his head.

'What?' I asked.

'Well, Adrian is doing well enough to have some time away from hospital, so he's going to be with us over Christmas.'

I looked at Arian and smiled. 'Christmas, huh? So, you'll be here for some of the summer, then?'

Adrian winked at me and nodded.

'And…' Mr Dean said.

'And…' Adrian added.

'And what?' I said, my voice rising.

Adrian laughed. 'You can tell her.'

Mr Dean beamed. 'Well, Adrian is, as of two days ago, a permanent member of our family.'

I looked at Adrian and frowned. 'What does that mean?'

'It means I'm going to be living with Uncle Steve and Aunty Vicki permanently. For good,' Adrian said.

'But what about your mum?' Why did Adrian look so happy? This hadn't been what he wanted!

'Mum is going to see about staying in Fairview for a bit once she's finished in rehab. You know what she's like—no promises. She's lost her job and her apartment, so there's nothing to keep her in Chinderah anymore. But, regardless of what Mum does, I'm going to keep living with Uncle Steve and Aunty Vicki. Them, and your family too, have shown me what a home is. I still love my mum, but living with her isn't what I want. This is what I want.'

I threw my arms around Adrian. 'And you're sure?'

Adrian laughed. 'I've never been so sure of anything. Uncle Steve has even offered Tom a room, should he ever want it.'

I smiled. 'It's all working out then.'

Adrian nodded.

'So, Fred,' I whispered as Mrs Anderson began asking everyone to return to their seats for the speeches. 'Have you got any big trips planned for next year, once you're free from all your hospital duties?'

'Well, I've been thinking about what you said, and wouldn't mind a trip to Vietnam. There was an amazing article on a river cruise you can do along Ha Long bay in that magazine you got me. They have a Madam Tussauds in Vietnam too, you know. Always wanted to go to one of those.'

'You know there is one of them on the Gold Coast, don't you?'

Adrian laughed. 'No, I didn't, but Vietnam sounds a bit more exotic, don't you think?'

Laughter burned in my chest until I let it escape. From the corner of my eye, Adrian was smiling a big, goofy smile.

'Can I come along on one of your journeys sometime, do you think?'

Adrian's blue eyes were bright and alive. 'Of course. I wouldn't dream of going without you.' He picked up my hand and kissed the back of it.

Mr Dean began moving chairs to create an easier path for Adrian to get through. I let go of his hand so he could move the wheelchair himself, placing my hand on his shoulder instead.

'You know what?' Adrian looked up at me. 'We have the rest of our lives to explore this amazing world. Right now, I'm happy to just hang around here.' He took his hoodie from the back of the wheelchair and, manoeuvering himself towards a small bin, he placed the hoodie in it as he rolled past.

Acknowledgements

A special thank you to Rochelle Manners and the rest of the Rhiza Press team for taking me on as a new author, and especially to the ever-patient Emily Lighezzolo; thanks for doing the hard work of making me say less than I always seem to think I need to say.

To my family: Larry, you have continued to smile and say yes to all my crazy dreams—and then made my dreams ours. You are my hero who holds my arms up when I get weary. To Emily, who inspires me every day with her thoughtfulness and determination; to Anna whose sweet heart makes my heart smile; and Molly, our treasure.

To my parents, Jim and Elaine, who have encouraged me in my writing for over 30 years.

Where would a girl be without her best friends? Kelly, Jax and Michelle, you've kept me sane by praying for me, having coffees with me, driving my kids around, reminding me to not give up on this dream, and generally making life beautiful.

To my first teenage readers, Sarah-Louise, Nikki and Lillian—I'll be forever grateful for the enthusiasm and encouragement after reading my story.

To my NaNoWriMo buddies, Jennifer and Caroline, who read the manuscript as I wrote it, and to all those wonderful friends who gave me feedback at some point along the journey.

Finally, to the Australian Christian writing community I have come to value so much—Omega Writers, Christian Writers Downunder and Australasian Christian Writers—thank you for sharing your knowledge and wisdom with the online world.

www.ingramcontent.com/pod-product-compliance
Lightning Source LLC
LaVergne TN
LVHW010056110826
845155LV00028B/365

* 9 7 8 1 9 2 5 5 6 3 2 0 7 *